The Adventure of the Bloody Duck
and other tales of Sherlock Holmes

By

Margaret Walsh

Editor – David Marcum

Paperback ISBN 978-1-78705-996-2
ePub ISBN 978-1-78705-997-9
PDF ISBN 978-1-78705-998-6

Published by MX Publishing
335 Princess Park Manor, Royal Drive,
London, N11 3GX
www.mxpublishing.co.uk

Cover design by Brian Belanger

To

**Margie Deck, Nancy Holder, David Marcum,
David Ruffle, and Andrea Williams**

Contents

Foreword

Sometime during 2021, during an exchange of emails with David Marcum, he suggested that I consider putting together an anthology of my stories. At the time I put it off as I was busy working on my fourth novel, *Sherlock Holmes and the Curse of Neb-Heka-Ra*.

As the year progressed it became horribly clear that, due to the sheer volume of research, the book would not be ready for publication in 2022. I tentatively reached out to Steve Emecz at MX Publishing and asked if an anthology would be acceptable for this year. He agreed and I turned my attention to the short stories I had written.

It also became clear that I did not have enough previously published work to make a reasonable anthology, so I set about writing two new stories for the book. In this anthology you will find four previously published stories, two new ones written expressly for this book. There is also a short essay at the end that I wrote to explain why Sherlock Holmes had such a grip on me.

Each story has an introduction explaining where each story was originally published, who the editor was, and any small snippets of information that you may find interesting. Feel free to flick over those if such things do not interest you.

Enjoy!

Margaret Walsh

Melbourne, Australia, January 2022.

Introduction: The Adventure of the Bloody Duck

'The Adventure of the Bloody Duck' was a story that I wrote simply to get an idea out of my mind. I had come across a reference in a true crime book about a murder in New York State in the 19th century that involved a blood-stained duck. I could not resist taking the idea and giving it a Sherlock Holmes twist.

This story first appeared in "The MX Book of New Sherlock Holmes Stories Part XXVI: 2021 Annual 1889-1897". The story was edited by David Marcum.

The Adventure of the Bloody Duck

I had seen many strange things in my time living in 221B Baker Street with Mr. Sherlock Holmes, but an elderly man standing in the middle of our living room holding a blood-stained duck was most certainly one of the oddest of my experiences.

The adventure began on a morning on a cold, crisp, early December day. It had snowed over the previous few days, blanketing London in a soft, white, shawl. The city looked pristine, and coldly beautiful, at least at a distance.

Holmes and I had been reading the newspapers and discussing a particularly vicious robbery that had resulted in the murder of a railway guard on the St Albans to London train that had occurred three days previously. I was of the opinion that the rogues would not be found, due to the inclement weather conditions. Holmes, of course, held a differing view. Our somewhat lively debate was interrupted by Mrs. Hudson knocking upon our door.

She ushered a man in, patted his shoulder reassuringly, smiled at us briefly, and left.

The elderly, white-haired, pink-cheeked, gentleman stood in our doorway, clutching a bird to his chest. A quick glance told me that the bird was a duck. A much longer look showed that the gentleman was somewhat nervous, the duck less so.

Holmes examined him without saying a word, but with gently raised eyebrows. The gentleman, seemingly nervous of the scrutiny, blurted out "I went to the police, Mr. Holmes, but they just laughed at me. They said Albert must have got into water where someone had been gutting fish." He waved the duck in our direction.

"Albert?" I asked, more than a little confused.

"I do believe Albert is the duck, Watson, or, more accurately, the drake," Holmes said.

Holmes rose from his chair, walked over and carefully examined the duck with his magnifying glass. "It is indeed blood, but rather too much of it to be fish blood." He smiled at the man and gestured to a chair. "Please sit down Mr...?"

"Sebastian Staines, Mr. Holmes, Doctor Watson. I live out at Highgate. I am retired from banking in the City. I bought a little house with a garden. I got Albert and another couple of ducks to both supply me with eggs and eat the pests that eat my vegetables. Albert is the only one of the birds that likes to wander, but he does not go far." Staines smiled a little nervously. "My neighbour, Rupert Dander, has a slightly bigger house than mine and lets rooms to single men. Albert tends to wander over there because Dander gives him seed cake. This morning, one of the lodgers damn near threw Albert over the fence at me and told me to keep him home, or he would end up as dinner. I was quite upset as you can imagine, so it was not until I got inside that I really looked at Albert." He looked down at the duck which was sitting placidly in his lap looking for all the world like a feathered cat. "That is when I noticed the blood. And then I thought it odd that one of the lodger's would return my duck. Dander never bothers. He lets Albert come and go as he pleases."

"How long has Mr. Dander had this particular lodger?" Holmes asked.

"Two new lodgers arrived about two days ago. Couple of unpleasant looking chaps. Not ruffians, you understand," Staines hastened to assure us, "…but cold eyed, and after the threat to poor Albert, I would say cold-hearted as well."

"Indeed. Your neighbour is named Rupert Dander, you say?"

The gentleman nodded.

Holmes sat back in his chair, a frown of concentration on his face. He looked at our visitor. "Well, Mr. Staines, you have interested me immensely. I suggest you take Albert home and keep him safe indoors for a while. I shall make some enquiries."

After obtaining the man's address, Holmes politely showed our visitor to the door, before turning to me with a slight smile. "Well, what do you make of that, Watson?"

"A duck, Holmes? Really?"

"A crime detecting duck is tad unusual, I will admit," my friend said dryly.

"Crime detecting?"

"Oh yes. I do believe our little feathered friend has stumbled upon a murder." Holmes looked across at the newspaper he had been reading before Mr. Staines had arrived, a slight frown creasing his brows.

"Murder, Holmes?" I asked, aghast.

"Oh yes!" He picked up the newspaper and handed it to me, before putting on his hat and coat and heading out the door. "I need to check upon a few people, then we shall head to Highgate."

"Holmes..."

Holmes paused in the doorway. His face was shuttered and expressionless. "I know the name Rupert Dander," he said softly. "He was a superintendent with the London Metropolitan Police. Dander retired not long after I began my career as a consulting detective."

Holmes walked out, shutting the door behind him, and I looked down, somewhat bewildered, at the newspaper story about the train robbery that had resulted in a murder. What this had to do with the old man, his pet duck, and a retired police superintendent, I simply could not fathom.

It was late afternoon before Holmes returned. He hummed contentedly to himself as he warmed his hands before the fire. "Well, Watson," he said cheerfully, "How do you feel about a little visit to Highgate tomorrow?"

"We are going to see a man about a duck, I take it?"

Holmes chuckled lightly at my pathetic sally. "Oh yes indeed, and we will have one or two people accompanying us."

"Anyone I know?" I asked.

"I visited Scotland Yard and had a little chat with Athelney Jones. He does not agree with my conclusions, but he will accompany us to Highgate."

"Does he ever agree with your conclusions?" Amusement coloured my tone.

"On very rare occasion," Holmes replied. "The name Rupert Dander, however, at least motivated him to listen."

The next morning, we stepped outside to find Inspector Athelney Jones was waiting for us, accompanied by several younger detectives who sat nearby in one of a pair of growlers.

"I'm still not sure about this, Mr. Holmes," said Jones. "I think the old man is barking, or you are."

"Indeed not, Inspector. Come now, it is a pleasant day for a short excursion to Highgate, followed by a brisk walk. You will follow my lead, I trust."

"I'll follow." Athelney Jones sighed. "I think you're quite mad. Lord knows what that makes me."

"A police officer doing his duty, my fine fellow."

Athelney Jones sighed again as we boarded the growler. "I just hope this doesn't turn out to be a wild goose chase."

"No geese involved. A duck, yes, but no geese need apply." Holmes settled back into his seat in high good humour as the horses pulled us away.

The rather charming village of Highgate is situated near the north-eastern corner of Hampstead Heath. People of reasonable means have chosen to retire here, for both its salubrious environs and its relative closeness to London. Highgate Cemetery, with its beautiful and ornate grave ornaments, was considered an excellent place to take a pleasant stroll on a Sunday.

Once we arrived in Highgate, Holmes led the way to one of the local pubs. Waving to us to wait outside, he slipped inside, and I noticed him chatting briefly with a man I took to be the landlord. Holmes gave the man a few coins and re-joined us outside.

"According to the landlord, Mr. Dander has not been seen for two days."

"Could be any number of reasons for that, Mr. Holmes. None of them felonious," said Jones.

"Quite."

I could see that Holmes was beginning to get irritated with Athelney Jones.

"Mr. Dander usually takes a walk around Pond Square of an evening, but, as I said, he has not been seen. The landlord's wife went to check up on him only this morning and was treated quite nearly as rudely as Mr. Staines," continued Holmes.

"What are we to do?" I asked.

Holmes smiled grimly. "First of all, I think I shall call upon Mr. Dander and see who answers the door. Watson, you will come with me. Inspector Jones, find a place where you can see the door, but not be seen. Coming, Watson?"

We walked towards a row of houses situated just off Pond Square. Pond Square was named for the two ponds that had supplied fresh drinking water to Highgate but had been drained several years ago to create a public space. The houses nearby were, consequently, much sort after.

Athelney Jones concealed himself beneath an overhanging tree, along with the youngest of the detectives. The rest of the detectives remained in Pond Square, and Holmes and I headed towards the house.

"Jones does not believe there has been a murder committed, does he, Holmes?" I paused. "Would it not have been better to bring Lestrade?" I asked.

Holmes snorted. "Believe me, Watson, if Lestrade had been available I would have prevailed upon him to accompany us. Unfortunately, he is engaged in discovering who murdered the mistress of a minor politician. It was her former lover, of course, the flowers in the parlour told me that, but Lestrade is chasing down every possible person who saw her on the day of her death. Gregson is out of the city at the moment, holidaying in Margate, I am led to understand, so that left me with one of the inspectors I have not worked with, or with Jones. Jones, whilst being an idiot on this occasion, is, at least, a known factor, and relatively willing to listen."

We walked on in silence to a tall, slightly rundown, house, which appeared to have been erected during the reign of one of the Georges. The houses on either side where much better kept, giving the house in question the air of a down at the heels companion to a pair of middle-aged maiden aunts.

An ornate wrought-iron fence with a small gate stood between the front door and the world at large.

Before placing his hand on the small gate, Holmes cast an eye over the pathway leading to the door. The pathway comprised brightly coloured tiles, that although faded and worn, showed beneath the thin layer of snow that covered them. I could make no sense of the swirls upon the snow, but I did note the marks of small, daintily shod, feet amongst the strange patterns. Holmes nodded to himself, opened the gate, and went to the door, where he rapped firmly upon it. There was silence for a moment, before heavy footsteps came to the door. A surly chap, with cold blue eyes glared out at us.

"What do you want?"

"Mr. Braddon at the pub tells me that you have rooms to let." Holmes's voice was almost a whine. "I am looking to take a break from the vile air of London."

"Ain't no rooms to be had. Go away!" The door was slammed in our faces.

'Such charming manners," Holmes observed drily, as he turned back to where I waited at the gate. We walked away, collected Jones, and then joined the other detectives in Pond Square.

Athelney Jones was shaking his head doubtfully. "It looks like him, Mr. Holmes, but I wasn't close enough to get a really good look."

"I think we can get you close enough for that," Holmes replied. He gestured to the detective who had accompanied Jones to his vantage point, a man named Harrison, to join us. "You saw which house I went to?"

"Yes, sir," Harrison replied.

"Well, go to the one just before it and talk to Mr. Staines. I need you to ask him three questions: does Mr. Dander have a compost heap, and if so, is there snow upon it, and is there any damage to Mr. Dander's drainpipes."

The young detective nodded and shot away. Both Jones and I gave Holmes odd looks. Holmes smiled grimly and said, "Mr. Braddon at the pub told me that Mr. Dander had had a fine, new, water heater installed recently and plumbing to remove the water from the bath."

"I do not understand you, Mr. Holmes, so help me..." Athelney Jones complained.

"Do not fret, Inspector, all we become clear – sooner rather than later, I do believe."

I watched Harrison knock upon Mr. Staines door, introduce himself, and be admitted. I turned to Holmes. "Why on earth did you send Harrison to Staines? Surely we could have gone next door and asked him ourselves?"

Holmes gave me an irritated look. "Think, Watson! If we had done that, and we were being watching by the charming individual we spoke to at Dander's house, our chickens would have flown the coop before we had even crossed the road."

Constable Harrison was in the house only a few minutes before returning.

He came panting up to us. "Mr. Holmes, the gentleman says that his neighbour does have a compost heap and there is no snow upon it. But he cannot see the drainpipes from his rear garden for they are on the other side of the house."

Holmes shrugged. "No matter. Ah well! It would have been nice to have confirmation, but the state of the compost heap is confirmation enough."

"You are not making sense, Mr. Holmes," Inspector Jones complained again. I've said it before, I am very much afraid you have brought us on a wild goose chase."

"All will be revealed shortly, inspector. Come, Watson, you and I will call upon Mr. Staines. Jones, give us ten minutes to get into position before you break down the door of Mr. Dander's house."

"I'm trusting you, Mr. Holmes. If you're wrong…"

"I am not wrong!" With a sniff, Holmes turned away from the inspector, beckoned to me, and we went up the road to Mr. Staines house.

"Inspector Jones is not a happy man," I observed.

"Athelney Jones is impatient," Holmes retorted. "He will be happy with the outcome soon enough."

Mr. Staines saw us coming and opened the door as we approached.

The old man was quite puzzled when he let us in. "Such strange questions that police detective asked me, Mr. Holmes."

"Do not fear, Mr. Staines, all will be made clear in a few minutes time. Now, if my good friend and I could make free of your rear garden I would be much obliged."

Mr. Staines led the way down the hallway and into a warm, flag-stoned, kitchen, and opened a door leading outside.

We were shown out to a tidy little garden, with a pen for the ducks, and banked earth showing where vegetables would be planted in the spring. A fence of middling height divided the garden from that of Mr. Dander's.

Holmes crouched below the level of the wall, indicating that I join him. "I was a trifle worried that the wall would be a little high to climb if needs be. But I think we shall neither of us have difficulty getting over this one should the need arise."

"You are anticipating we shall need to?"

"Only if Jones and the other detectives fail to act with necessary swiftness."

We crouched in silence for a few minutes. It was cold and uncomfortable, and I could feel my knees stiffening.

Then noise erupted from the house next door. There was much banging, loud thumps, roars of fury, and mighty oaths, of the like I had not heard since I was in the army. Holmes rose to his feet and leaned against the fence. I struggled to my feet and joined him. There was movement in the house but none in the garden. I looked around and spotted the compost heap that Holmes had evinced such an interest in. The greenish black mound looked almost obscene against the pristine, cool, whiteness of the snow.

Athelney Jones opened the rear door, a beaming smile stretching from ear to ear across his face. "I don't know how you did it, Mr. Holmes, but this is a beauty of a collar. The Yard owes you. Come and join us."

I looked at Holmes. "Are we going over the fence?"

"I think we shall enter through the front door like civilized men, Watson."

We went back through Mr. Staines house and were met at the front of the next house by the sight of the man who had answered the door, and another being dragged away in handcuffs.

"Have your men dig through the compost, inspector, you will find the remains of Mr. Dander concealed within," Holmes said.

The two arrested felons, turned their heads, eyes wild, at my friend's pronouncement.

Ignoring them, Holmes continued into the house, and out the back to the garden we had gazed across the wall at. Behind me I could hear Athelney Jones shouting orders to fetch rakes and mattocks.

Holmes did not spare the compost heap even a glance as he headed around the other side of the house. He stopped and made a sound of satisfaction, pointing at a frozen, somewhat mucky, puddle on the ground, and a broken drainpipe.

Shouts from the yard made us both turn around. Athelney Jones came towards us. "You were right, Mr. Holmes. There's a body cut up and concealed in the compost pile. How you knew this, I don't rightly know. It's like witchcraft, it is."

Holmes snorted. "Hardly that. Merely reasoning and observation."

Athelney Jones turned away shouting for bags to put the remains in. Holmes and I quietly took our leave. As the growlers now had to transport two prisoners, Holmes and I walked through the snow to the station and home to Baker Street.

I had got chilled to the bone crouching in the snow-covered garden. Upon our return to Baker Street, I bundled myself up in blankets and curled up in my chair before the fire, a glass of brandy in my hand. I looked across at Holmes who was similarly arranged.

After a long moment of silence I said "I do not understand what happened."

"Simplicity itself, my dear Watson."

"To you, most certainly, but not to me. I am quite bewildered as to how the outcome of the case was reached."

Holmes smiled slightly and set his snifter of brandy down on the table beside him. "When we got to Dander's house it was obvious that the landlord's wife had been the only person near the front door in several days. The marks of her shoes and the hem of her dress were the only marks in the snow. No other feet had trod there."

"But the water heater, and the drainpipe, and, good heavens, Holmes, the compost heap? Not to mention what the duck has to do with it all."

'The duck was the first clue. Upon examining its feathers, it became clear that the blood had got upon the creature from bathing in it, not splashed upon him from above. The underside of his wings, and his belly were stained with blood. Once the landlord told me about the water heater, all became clear."

"Not to me it isn't," said Athelney Jones from the doorway.

"Come in, Jones. Sit down." Holmes waved the inspector to a seat. I unwound myself from my blankets to fetch the inspector a brandy.

"The water heater?" I asked.

"Water heaters are attached to a bathtub that has drainage built in. The plumbing necessary to run one requires a bath that empties automatically by the means of removing a plug, rather than dragging the bath outside to empty it. As such it is the perfect place to dismember a corpse without making too much of a mess. Water will simply wash the blood away."

Holmes took a sip of his brandy. "The volume of water required to perform that task, however, is considerably more than that used for the average bath. The plumbing, new as it was, could not stand up to the increased pressure, and ruptured, causing a puddle of warm, blood-stained water, to form below the broken pipe."

"Which Albert bathed in!" I exclaimed, the light dawning.

Jones blinked. "The duck's name is Albert? How very patriotic."

"Indeed." Holmes' tone was dry. "The cold meant that disposing of the corpse would prove difficult. The ground would be much too hard to dig. Hence my question about the compost heap. Much easier to remove several layers of compost, place the remains in there, and then replace the compost. But, of course, there was no way to replace the snow that had been upon the heap."

"But who and why?" I asked.

"If I may, Mr. Holmes?" Athelney Jones asked.

Holmes waved his hand to indicate permission.

"Four days ago, there was an attempted robbery on the St Albans to London train, carried out by two men, who killed the guard on duty, but got very little money for their trouble. Mr. Holmes came to me yesterday saying he knew where they were holed up.," said Jones.

I thought for a moment. "Mr. Dander's new lodgers? Did the gentleman realize who they were?"

Holmes was silent for a moment. "We will never know for certain. But Mr. Rupert Dander certainly knew a bad man when he saw one. And he had seen a lot - he was a retired superintendent of Scotland Yard, as you already know."

"But how would the robbers know that?" I asked.

"There was a daguerreotype of Dander in uniform upon the wall in the front parlour. He was much younger in it, but it would have been obvious that it was the same man," said Jones.

Jones then got to his feet. "Thank you, gentlemen, for your assistance. The Yard is grateful that you helped capture these villains. I admit that we would not have caught them on our own."

"Do not thank us, inspector," said Holmes. "You owe the swift capture of those murderous thugs to one small duck."

Jones smiled. "Should we give the duck some small token of our appreciation?"

"I believe Albert is partial to seed cake," Holmes replied, with a glimmer of a smile. Jones laughed and left.

Holmes continued "Just as I am partial to a little roast duck, but I fear on this occasion it would not be appropriate. What say you to roast beef at Simpsons, Watson?"

"An excellent proposition, Holmes."

"Come then, a little dinner and then the Philharmonic Society at St James Hall, will quite round off the evening, don't you think?"

"A capital notion," I replied. Getting to my feet and reaching for my coat and hat.

Snow was falling again as we walked down Baker Street into the wintery evening.

Introduction: The Affair of the Helingstone Rubies

This was the first of my stories to be accepted for David Marcum's prestigious anthologies. I was shocked when David approached me about submitting a story. Having just had my first novel published, I admit that I was still very unsure of my writing abilities.

The anthology this story appeared in originally was "The MX Book of New Sherlock Holmes Stories – Part XXIII: Some More Untold Cases (1888-1894)" in 2020.

The anthology contained various author's attempts at explaining the unwritten stories of Sir Arthur Conan Doyle, such as the famous Giant Rat of Sumatra.

The Affair of the Helingstone Rubies

It was a warm summer's afternoon when the messenger came from Mycroft Holmes that led us into one of the strangest cases of my long association with Mr. Sherlock Holmes.

I was once more residing in our rooms in Baker Street, as my wife had ventured to the countryside to nurse an ill friend. Holmes and I had slid back into our congenial relations of old and were perusing the newspapers when the messenger arrived.

It seemed there was nothing in the papers except for reports the extraordinary jewel thefts from Calcroft House in Dorset. It was a puzzle, I felt, that would interest Holmes, but so far he had shown little inclination to pursue it, nor had his assistance been sought. That was about to change.

The young man that Mrs. Hudson showed to our door was dressed in the livery of the Diogenes Club. He handed the envelope he was carrying to Holmes without a word. Holmes read the contents then looked at the lad. "Tell my brother that we shall be there as requested."

The lad nodded, turned around and marched out of our rooms.

I looked to where Holmes had carelessly discarded the missive. It bore Mycroft's distinctive handwriting and simply read: "*Diogenes Club. Six o'clock.*"

"Short and to the point, eh Watson?"

"Not very informative," I agreed.

Holmes glanced at the clock. "Well, we haven't long to wait." With that he returned to reading the papers and, after a moment, I did the same.

At six o'clock precisely we arrived at the Diogenes Club and were shown into the Stranger's Room, where Mycroft was waiting for us, along with a tall, well-dressed man with dark blonde hair and well-trimmed beard, and with a worried, careworn, expression on his otherwise handsome face.

"Sherlock! Doctor! Good of you both to come." Mycroft handed us both a glass of brandy and waved us to the chairs set out for us. The unknown man was already seated, toying absently with his own glass of brandy.

Mycroft took his seat before saying, "This is Percival Calcroft, M.P. He has a problem that needs your skills, Sherlock."

"You mean the mysteriously disappearing jewellery." Holmes said.

I noted that the man, Percival Calcroft, flinched perceptibly at Holmes's words.

"Indeed," Mycroft said.

"Why are you interesting yourself in jewel thefts, Brother, no matter how mysterious?" Holmes asked. His tone was curious. "After all, it is hardly a matter of grave importance to Her Majesty's Government."

"Not to Her *Government*," Mycroft agreed.

Holmes looked sharply at his brother. "But of importance to Her *Majesty*?"

Mycroft nodded. "The last theft was of a ruby necklace – "

"The Helingstone Rubies," I said, pleased to be able to add something to the conversation. "It was in the paper today. A matched necklace of exquisite blood red rubies. "

Mycroft nodded. "The necklace was gifted to Her Majesty by the late Colonel Bertram Helingstone. Her Majesty had loaned the necklace to a distant cousin of hers to wear at a ball at Calcroft House."

Percival Calcroft groaned and placed his head in his hands. "I am ruined!"

"When was the necklace last seen?" Holmes asked.

"Just before the ball," Calcroft replied, his voice muffled by his hands. "Lady Alexandrina's maid had taken the necklace from its safety box and placed in on the dressing table prior to dressing her mistress. The girl was called into another part of the suite to fetch something for her mistress. When she came back, the necklace had gone."

"No one came to the suite?"

Calcroft raised his head. "No, Mr. Holmes. Nor could anyone have got into the room via the windows. Lady Alexandrina had the Coral Suite on the fourth floor. The window was open to catch the sea breeze, but no one could possibly have climbed up the wall. They would have been seen, for one thing."

"Interesting," Holmes commented.

"Will you take the case, Sherlock?" Mycroft asked.

"When I thought it to be simply a case of jewel theft, I would have said no," Holmes admitted. "But your story intrigues me greatly."

"You will come to Calcroft House?" Percival Calcroft was almost pathetically eager.

"I will come." Holmes looked at me, eyebrows raised.

"And I also," I said. "If you think I can be of use to you, Holmes," I added.

"I doubt there will ever be a time when you are not of use to me, my friend." He turned to his brother. "Can you get me a list of all the other jewellery that has also been stolen?"

Mycroft took a folded sheet of paper from his pocket and handed it to his brother without comment.

Holmes tucked into his own jacket pocket. "I shall study this at my leisure. Mr. Calcroft, if it suits you, Watson and I will come down to Calcroft House in a day or so."

"Certainly, Mr. Holmes." Percival Calcroft looked as if a great weight had been removed from his shoulders. "You can take the train to Swanage and I will send a carriage to collect you from the station. Calcroft House is near Worth Matravers, which is west of Swanage. A cab would bring you out, but it would cost you a fortune."

The man got to his feet, now smiling, and with a definite spring in his step, took his leave from us.

When he had gone, Mycroft looked at his brother. "Thank you, Sherlock. Her Majesty is most upset."

Holmes waved a hand in a self-deprecating manner. "The puzzle interests me, Mycroft, no more than that. Pray do not read any unnecessary altruistic motives into my agreement." He looked more closely at his brother. "What do you know about the inhabitants of Calcroft House?"

"Apart from Percival Calcroft, there is his wife, Annabelle. She is the youngest daughter of Lord Aubrey Derwent. No children." Mycroft paused to gather his thoughts. "The other permanent resident is Percival's younger brother, Peregrine. Peregrine was a bit of a scapegrace as a youngster. Went to Asia to make his fortune."

"And did he?" Holmes asked.

Mycroft nodded. "He came back with a fortune made from trading in Oriental art from China and Japan, and he continues to deal in artworks on the Continent. Peregrine travels several times a year to France."

"Interesting," Holmes commented, "But probably not useful."

We took our leave from Mycroft and headed out into the gathering dusk. Holmes was in a hurry to return home, so, much to my regret, we hailed a cab rather than walk. I felt it a great pity. Whilst London can be dangerous, and is almost always noxious, there are few places as pleasant to walk about in as the capital on a pleasant summer's evening.

Back in the Baker Street rooms, Holmes settled himself in to study the list that Mycroft had supplied to him. I contented myself with finishing the newspapers that I had begun before our summons.

Finally, Holmes threw the papers onto the table with a sigh.

I looked up. "Did you gain anything?"

"Not a thing, except for the fact that the pieces taken were all quite large. Heavy necklaces and bracelets."

I frowned. "Wouldn't those be the logical things to take?"

Holmes shook his head. "Too hard to smuggle out of the house. Jewel thieves tend to take things that are easily concealable, such as rings and ear-rings, or even tie-pins. Things that can be tucked into coat linings without creating a noticeable bulge." He looked across at me. "This case should prove to be extremely interesting."

Holmes spent the next day finding out what he could about the occupants of Calcroft House from sources other than Mycroft, though he was not inclined to share his information with me. Due to his reluctance to confide in me I suspected that what little he had found had come from Langdale Pike.

Langdale Pike – not his real name, you can be quite sure of that – was a society gossip-monger of whom I disapproved. Gossip has never interested me and I find the mere idea of dealing in it as if it was some form of commodity extremely distasteful. Holmes had no such reluctance. Indeed I suspected his friendship with Pike, if that is what it was, predated his friendship with me. At this remove, I'm prepared to admit that there may have been a slight tinge of jealousy in my attitude towards Pike.

The day after that we woke early and headed to Waterloo Station to catch a London and South Western Railway service to Swanage. The train took us through Surrey and through England's ancient capital of Winchester. We couldn't go directly to Swanage – the Dorchester line on which we were traveling bypassed it. We alighted at Wareham and got on a branch service that took us to Swanage.

It was originally little more than a fishing village, and a supplier of fine Purbeck marble, but under the encouragement of local businessmen John Mowlem and George Burt, it had flourished into a charming tourist town akin to Eastbourne. There were more than a few people on the branch line train, and the platform was extremely crowded when we arrived.

Gathering our luggage, we hastened out of the station. I paused to breathe in the cool, crisp, sea air. Holmes was looking around for Percival Calcroft's coachman. As it turned out, Calcroft himself came to meet us. I spotted him striding towards us.

He held out his hand to both of us. "Thank you for coming, gentlemen." We were led to where a fine carriage waited nearby. The coachmen loaded our luggage and we joined Calcroft inside. It took him a while to extract us from the crowd around the station, but we soon set off at a brisk pace out of town.

"I thought it best to come with Alfred," Calcroft said, a wave of his hand indicating that Alfred was the coachman. "With the nice weather bringing so many people out, I felt he wouldn't easily find you. I, at least, have the advantage of knowing what you both look like."

Calcroft was practically beaming with delight. "I cannot tell you how relieved I am that you've both come. Everything will be all right now." His childlike confidence in my friend was as endearing as it was worrying.

Holmes held up a hand. "As my good friend Watson here will tell you, I'm not infallible. There is no guarantee that I'll find the jewel thief, though if I can discover how the thefts are carried out, then I'll know who is responsible."

"Just your being here, Mr. Holmes, takes a great weight off my mind," Percival Calcroft replied.

We passed through the village of Worth Matravers. It was a pretty place, with cottages and farm houses constructed out of limestone built around a large duck pond. It was the sort of place that poets tend to call idyllic. The people seemed prosperous and content. More than one waved cheerfully when they spotted the coach.

Once through the village, the carriage swung off the main road and bounced down a slightly less-well-maintained one. We passed through a charming wooded park, and I could tell that we were heading towards the sea. As we came out through the trees, I gaped in astonishment at the sight that met my eyes. A large manor house sat on a prominent position near the cliffs. It was built of some light-coloured stone that gleamed in the sunlight. It was so bright that it almost hurt to look upon it.

Calcroft noticed my reaction and chuckled softly. "That is Calcroft House, Doctor Watson. What do you think of it?"

To be truthful, I couldn't see it clearly enough to form an opinion, honest or otherwise.

"It is certainly bright," Holmes commented.

"The locals call it Calcroft's Lighthouse, or simply, the Light House, because of the way it reflects the sunlight," Calcroft said. "My great-great-grandfather built it out of local limestone and chert. It has more than the usual number of windows as well. He wanted plenty of light and sea air inside. I believe he was troubled by his chest. At least, that's what my father said." He gave the house a look that was almost affectionate. "It is a monster to heat in the winter, but the rest of the year it's pleasant enough."

The carriage drew up in front of the building, which was, thankfully, not nearly so bright as when one was close to it.

We climbed down from the carriage and Calcroft took us inside, where his wife was waiting to greet us, along with a man, who by his resemblance to our host, I took to be his brother, Peregrine. Introductions were made and the butler, a stiff-spined, stone-faced individual by the name of Hopkins, showed us to our rooms on the third floor.

The room I was given was spacious, bright, and airy. I saw what Percival Calcroft meant about an unusual number of windows. The exterior wall was comprised almost entirely of several extremely large windows that gave out onto views of the English Channel. The air was filled with the cries of sea birds, and I noted that there seemed to be a colony of shags or cormorants, along with seagulls and terns, making their homes on the cliff and in the rocks below.

Hopkins tapped upon my door and I accompanied him back downstairs, where we joined the Calcrofts in a comfortable parlour where tea was waiting. I allowed Hopkins to serve me a cup of tea and a selection of sandwiches, and settled back into a well-upholstered chair.

It was then that I observed the presence of another person: A well-dressed young woman with dark hair, brown eyes that sparkled with merriment, and a well-placed dimple, who sat beside Mrs. Calcroft. She was introduced to us as Miss Cynthia Taverner, the cousin of a colleague of our host who had come to Dorset for the benefit of her health. I couldn't forebear raising my eyebrows. In truth, there seemed to be little, if anything, actually wrong with the woman. She appeared to be the picture of rude health. I looked at Holmes who, when our hosts weren't looking, winked at me. I made a mental note to myself to ask him what he knew about Miss Taverner, as he didn't seem at all surprised by her appearance.

After tea, our host excused himself and handed us over to his brother for a tour of the house. Holmes gave every appearance of being interested in the furnishings and ornaments, but I knew him well enough to know that all he was really interested in was solving the puzzle.

Peregrine Calcroft was a genial man, bluff and hearty, as he showed us around, and every inch the English country gentleman. "It's a fine house, what? A grand place for a lad to grow up, that is for sure." He beamed at me and swept his arm in a wide arc towards the cliffs. "Can you think of a finer place for a boy, Doctor Watson?"

"In truth, Mr. Calcroft, I cannot," I replied. "The sea air would be most beneficial."

We were standing just inside Peregrine Calcroft's own rooms, which were on the same floor as ours. He had shown us everywhere within the house, including the suite that comprised the personal apartments of his brother and his wife, which I for one, felt was a trifle odd. He had even dragged us through the servant's quarters.

Holmes had wandered towards the window and was staring at something just outside it. We joined him and I saw, with some puzzlement, that the object of Holmes's interest was a smallish wooden platform that had been affixed to the windowsill.

Holmes turned to Peregrine Calcroft with raised eyebrows.

The man fidgeted and looked faintly embarrassed. "I feed the squirrels, Mr. Holmes. They live in the trees in the park. But there isn't much food around for the poor things, so I help out a bit."

"That is very kind of you," I said into the awkward silence.

"Not very manly, though, is it, Doctor?" Peregrine said.

"I have never been one to subscribe to the theory that kindness is an exclusively feminine attribute," Holmes said. "Thank you for the tour, Mr. Calcroft. I think Watson and I will take a short walk before dinner." He turned and walked out of the room.

I hurriedly took my leave and hastened after Holmes.

It wasn't until we were walking in the park that I was able to get him to speak.

"What on earth was that about?"

"Hmm?"

"Your behaviour in Peregrine Calcroft's rooms was quite odd. Feeding squirrels on a platform outside his window may be unusual, but it is hardly a crime."

Holmes stopped and looked at me. "I may not know much about the natural world, Watson, but I do know one thing."

"What is that, Holmes?"

"Squirrels do not eat fish."

On that cryptic note he continued walking and refused to say another word on the subject.

I refused to allow Holmes's odd behaviour to disturb me. I walked beside him in the warm afternoon sunshine and found myself relaxing with the combination of gentle warmth and refreshing sea breeze. We walked for perhaps an hour, with Holmes pausing from time to time to examine a tree or two. I assumed he was looking for signs of squirrels and refrained from commenting. I was sure that if I said something, I would receive a statement along the lines of, "You see, but you do not observe".

We had turned back from the woods and by unspoken mutual agreement headed for the cliffs. The view was spectacular. If I squinted, I could discern a vague smudge on the horizon that I took to be France. I had to agree with Peregrine Calcroft – this was indeed a fine place for a boy to grow up. Relaxed and feeling somewhat content, regardless of the reason for our being here, I begin to whistle a merry air – an old Scots song: *"Charlie He's My Darling"*. It had always been a favourite of mine.

As we turned back towards the house, a flash of black swooped at me. I swore loudly and ducked as a large black bird came at me. Then it flew away. I admit I was shaken. Holmes came and stood beside me, gazing after the departing creature with an odd expression upon his face.

"God knows what possessed the blasted thing," I grumbled.

"Perhaps it didn't care for your whistling," Holmes said with a faint smile.

"An avian music critic?" I asked, brows raised.

The smile grew a hairs breadth wider. "There are stranger things, my friend, as we both well know."

I was in no mood now to continue with a walk. Holmes, sensing my mood, turned his steps back towards the house.

Even from close up, it was easy to see why the locals called it the Light House. In the late afternoon sun, it fairly gleamed. I was looking at the building and didn't notice Holmes stop and bend down and, as a consequence, I almost tripped over him.

Holmes straightened up and gave me an irritated look.

I glared at him. I was heading into an increasingly foul mood. I opened my mouth to snap at him, and then stopped when I perceived that he held something in his hand.

"What on earth is that?" I asked.

Holmes turned the object in his hand. It was a strip of leather, soft and worn smooth and tied in an odd loop. At one point the aged object had snapped, leaving the loop and two fraying ends. I was puzzled by it, but I failed to see why it held such interest for Holmes. "A bootlace?" I suggested, unable to think of any other purpose for a thin strip of worn leather.

Holmes tucked it into his pocket. "Not a bootlace, my dear Watson. A very valuable clue."

"A clue? You mean you already have an idea as to how these thefts have been carried out?" I was almost shocked. To my knowledge, we had seen nothing that could possibly lead us to the thief.

Holmes chuckled drily. "Indeed. It isn't even the first clue."

"Is it not? What was the first?"

"Squirrels," Holmes replied before walking on towards the house.

I stared after him, completely bemused. Holmes looked back over his shoulder. "Hurry along. We must change for dinner."

I swore to myself and then followed after him. There were times when Holmes was the most infuriating man on earth. This was one of them.

Dinner at Calcroft House was quite a formal affair, if somewhat unbalanced with men outnumbering the women. It took place in a formal dining room that showed signs of recent renovation. New drapes of burgundy velvet hung at the windows, and the table was draped in cloths of a matching shade.

The butler, Hopkins, and assorted footmen came and went with a number of excellent dishes. The main course was a fine Baron of Beef served with roasted potatoes, carrots and parsnips, green beans, and a rich, thick gravy. English cooking at its finest. Everyone paid due attention to their meal, and there was little talk until we reached the final stage of the meal, which was a cheese board comprising some quite excellent local cheeses.

I couldn't help but see that Miss Taverner, the woman who was staying there for her health, was wearing a rather large and ornate sapphire pendant. The jewel was the size of a quail's egg and set in a heavy mount of gold on a broad gold chain. To my mind it seemed a little out of keeping with the tone of the dinner to be wearing such an ostentatious piece.

Our host was eyeing the necklace almost nervously. "I do hope you have good strong box for that, Miss Taverner. I would be quite distraught should it be stolen. Not to mention embarrassed."

Miss Taverner laughed – a gay, tinkling sound. "Don't be concerned. I'll place it on my bedside table overnight and lock it away properly before I leave. It won't be out of my sight for long. Besides, isn't Mr. Holmes here to ensure no more jewels go missing?"

Holmes briefly acknowledged the conversation before cutting himself a wedge of a very fine Stilton, taking a small bite from it before turning to Peregrine Calcroft to say, "I understand you spent time in Asia."

"Why yes, Mr. Holmes. In both China and Japan. Both countries have produced some quite good artworks that have their admirers here."

"I have a familiarity with both countries," Holmes said which, I own, came as a complete surprise to me.

"Particularly around Linyi in Shandong Province in China," he continued, "and in Susaki in the Kochi Prefecture in Japan. Perhaps we may know people in common?"

Peregrine shook his head. "I'm afraid not, Mr. Holmes. In China I spent most of my time in Guilin in Guangxi Province, and in Japan I was in Asakura in Fukuoka Prefecture. Both are quite a reasonable distance from the places you mentioned." He smiled in a manner that was almost ingratiating. "But I would be delighted to hear of your adventures in those countries."

"Perhaps another time," Holmes demurred. "My reasons for being there weren't ones that are at all suitable to talk about in front of ladies." He nodded his head at our hostess and Miss Taverner.

"Another time then," Peregrine agreed.

The ladies withdrew from the table shortly afterwards, and we men went to the billiard room, except for Holmes, who pleaded fatigue and retired to bed. I saw that he stopped to have a word with a couple of the footmen before heading up the stairs. After several games of billiards with both our host and his brother, I too retired for the night.

Holmes and I were the first down for breakfast the next morning, though we were soon joined by Percival Calcroft and his wife. Good mornings were exchanged, but not another word was said as we helped ourselves to the food laid out in brightly polished silver chafing dishes on the sideboard.

I tucked into a plate of bacon, eggs, and devilled kidneys. Holmes filled his plate with coddled eggs and toast and sat beside me. I discerned that he didn't pay much attention to what he was eating. His entire focus was on the door to the breakfast room, which I thought was a little strange. I found myself watching the door as well, wondering exactly what it was that kept my friend's focus upon it. I wasn't kept in suspense for long.

Miss Taverner came to the door of the room and nodded briskly to Holmes. He got to his feet, startling our hosts.

"Is the breakfast not to your liking?" Calcroft asked.

"It is excellent, thank you. However, I think it's time that we apprehended the thief." Holmes pushed his chair back and walked to the door. After a moment of stunned silence, I followed, accompanied by Percival and Annabelle Calcroft.

Miss Taverner stood aside to let everyone out of the room and then followed us up the stairs.

Holmes led the way to a room that I recognized from the tour the previous day, that of Percival Calcroft's brother, Peregrine. Without so much as pausing to knock, Holmes threw the door open. Behind us I could hear Percival Calcroft's voice raised in complaint. How dare we intrude upon his brother! The complaints died as we all took in the scene in the room.

Peregrine Calcroft stood by the window gazing at us open-mouthed. In his left hand he held the sapphire pendant that Miss Taverner had been wearing the previous evening. In his right hand he held a fish – a fish that was taken from his unresisting hand by a large and decidedly impatient black bird that was sitting on the platform outside the open window.

Holmes strode across the room and took the sapphire from Peregrine's hand. The bird, not liking the crowd of humans around it, flew away towards the cliffs.

Peregrine Calcroft sank down onto his bed and placed his head in his hands, much as his brother had done in the Diogenes Club several days earlier.

Percival Calcroft stared at his brother. "Why?" His voice was anguished. "In God's name, why?"

Peregrine shook his head and wouldn't reply.

Holmes looked at me and tilted his head towards the door. I nodded and we quietly left the room, joining Miss Taverner in the hallway, where Holmes handed back the sapphire.

Annabelle Calcroft slipped into the room and stood staring at her brother-in-law, a comforting hand placed on her husband's shoulder.

Within the hour, Holmes and I, accompanied by Miss Taverner, had left the estate and were headed back to London.

It wasn't until several days later back in London, and in the comfortable confines of the Diogenes Club, that Holmes would deign to fully explain what had occurred. We were once again seated in the Stranger's Room with some of the club's excellent brandy.

"It was obvious," Holmes said, "that the thief had to be a member of the household. But not a servant."

"Why not a servant?" I asked.

"Too great a risk, Watson. Servant's belongings, and indeed their very persons, can be searched. In a situation like that, the only people who wouldn't be searched would be the family and guests. It was soon clear to me that it wasn't a guest."

Mycroft looked thoughtful. "Because there were never the same guests each time a theft occurred," he said.

"Exactly. Therefore, the thief had to be a member of the family. I thought it to be highly unlikely that an M.P. would be stealing from his guests. Nor his wife. Annabelle Calcroft's family is unusual amongst the English aristocracy: They are independently wealthy. Indeed, it was her father that financed her husband's run in politics. She is unlikely to be stealing jewels."

"Unless the poor lady suffers from kleptomania," I said.

Holmes waved his hand in a dismissive gesture. "Again, it is unlikely, though I admit I did consider the possibility. If that was the case, the kleptomania would most likely have manifested much earlier, and the lady's family would have placed her into an asylum rather than allow her to be married."

I thought about it for a moment, and then nodded. The class that Annabelle Calcroft belonged to was that which preferred to hide what it viewed as abnormalities behind high walls and securely locked doors. Holmes was correct. If Annabelle Calcroft had been a kleptomaniac, her father would never have permitted her to wed – and he certainly wouldn't have funded her husband's foray into politics, an arena where private lives had a tendency to become public ones.

"That left the brother, Peregrine," Mycroft observed.

I frowned. "But did he didn't make a fortune selling Asian artworks? What possible need could he have to steal?"

Holmes lips twisted into a wry smile. "He did indeed make a fortune, my dear Watson. He also spent it rather quickly."

"How do you know that?" I asked.

"You know that I have contacts in interesting places," Holmes replied.

"Including clubs in St. James Street," Mycroft murmured.

"Then I was correct in my surmise," I said. "You did go to Langdale Pike."

Holmes nodded. "I did. And a pretty tale he had to tell me about Peregrine Calcroft, involving expensive brothels and even more expensive gaming clubs. The money the fellow made didn't last long."

"But the method of the thefts? How on earth did you work them out?"

"The first clue was the platform outside Peregrine Calcroft's window."

I though back. "After we left his room, you made that odd comment about fish. I admit I didn't observe any fish upon the platform."

"There was no fish," Holmes said, "but there were fish scales caught along the edge of the platform. That was the first pointer that Calcroft's brother was the culprit."

"He took a calculated risk letting you into the room, Sherlock," Mycroft said.

"Peregrine really didn't have any choice," Holmes replied. "We had been given the grand tour of the house and been shown everywhere else. If he had left his own room out of the tour, it would have looked suspicious."

Mycroft nodded thoughtfully.

Holmes continued, "Several things combined to convince me that Peregrine Calcroft had trained a *Phalacrocorax carbo*, or Great Cormorant, not to catch fish, as they do in parts of Asia, but to steal jewels."

"And those things were?" Mycroft asked.

"The size of the pieces stolen. It was only large necklaces or pendants, with the occasional large bracelet. Nothing small, such as ear-rings or tie-pins."

Mycroft frowned for a moment then expression cleared. "Of course, the bigger pieces would be difficult for a bird to swallow."

"Exactly, and Peregrine Calcroft made certain of it by using a throat snare."

"A what?" I asked.

"A throat snare. That's what we found near the cliffs. It confirmed for me what I was already beginning to suspect, that thief was familiar with the practice of fishing with cormorants. Peregrine Calcroft confirmed it himself at dinner."

I frowned as I thought back to the dinner that night. I couldn't recall anything being said about fishing or cormorants, and I said so.

Holmes sighed. "The places where Peregrine Calcroft admitted to having spent a great deal of time: Guilin in Guangxi province in China, and Asakura in Fukuoka Prefecture in Japan – both areas where cormorant fishing is common."

"There is a great deal of difference between fishing and jewel theft," Mycroft observed. "One comes naturally to the bird – the other does not."

"Very true," Holmes agreed. "I cannot prove it, but though a traditional throat snare was used to prevent the bird ingesting the ill-gotten gains, I suspect other methods were used to train this bird. For example, it seems logical that a particular song was whistled to call the bird to him."

"What song?" I asked.

"'*Charlie He's my Darling*'," Holmes replied. "Or something very similar."

"The song that I was whistling when the bird almost hit me!" I exclaimed.

"I don't think it was going to hit you, Watson. I suspect that it was coming in to *land* on you, when the poor creature realized that you weren't its master, and flew away in confusion – another thing that led me to the conclusion a bird was involved was the windows and alcohol."

I gave Holmes a bewildered look, totally unable to follow his thought processes.

"A few questions to the servants after dinner led me to understand that the common factor amongst the thefts was that the owners of the stolen jewels had all been a little less than restrained about how much they drank at dinner, leading to a certain carelessness with their belongings, and that in every instance of theft, the windows had been left open."

"So Peregrine Calcroft trained the bird to fly into the rooms and remove jewellery that was sitting out in the open." I shook my head. "It's astounding. How on earth was the bird trained?"

"How isn't germane," Mycroft observed, before Holmes could reply. "The main thing is that the thief has been caught."

Holmes nodded. "With his brother moving so swiftly after the theft of the Helingstone Rubies, Peregrine Calcroft didn't have the opportunity to get away to sell them."

"Where was he selling them?" I asked. "Surely all the thefts were covered in the newspapers? Any reputable jeweller – "

Holmes chuckled drily. "You know as well as I do that all jewellers aren't reputable, my friend. You remember that Mycroft told us that Peregrine Calcroft journeyed several times a year to France – ostensibly to visit with the contacts he made in the art world, but I suspect it was actually to sell the jewels that he had stolen. He certainly came back from each trip with more money than he left with." His lips twisted back into the wry smile of earlier, "And there is no need to remind me that when Mycroft gave me the information, I was of the opinion that it was probably not of use."

I frowned as another thought struck me, on how lucky we were that Miss Taverner had been present. I said as much to Holmes and Mycroft.

Holmes snorted. "Luck, my dear fellow, had absolutely nothing to do with it. Miss Taverner is a private enquiry agent. Langdale Pike sent me her way when it became obvious that we would need to catch the thief red-handed.

"And the sapphire pendant?" I asked.

"It did not belong to Miss Taverner," Holmes replied. "A jeweller on Bond Street for whom she had done some good

work for in the past agreed to the loan of the item as bait."
Holmes smiled. "She really is the cousin of another M.P., who
was only too happy to help slide her into the household under
false pretenses."

"Freddie Taverner is game for just about anything,"
Mycroft commented.

"But what will happen now?" I asked. "Surely the scandal
will wreck Percival Calcroft's career?"

"There will be no scandal," Mycroft said firmly. "Peregrine
Calcroft has already left these shores, bound for Australia
accompanied by several stalwart footmen to ensure that he
doesn't disappear *en route*. Australia is still the place where
inconvenient and embarrassing relatives can be safely stashed.
He will not return. As for the jewels: The Helingstone Rubies
were recovered and Her Majesty is content for me to deal with
the thief in a manner that won't cause repercussions."

Mycroft turned his gaze on me. "It goes without saying,
Doctor Watson, that this case cannot be written about – much
less published."

I have adhered to Mycroft's command, but only in part. I
have written up the case but I have refrained from publishing it.
If it is ever published, it shall be long after all the participants
are dead and well beyond fear of scandal. Indeed, it is likely that
beyond being a mere curiosity what I have taken to calling "The

Helingstone Rubies" will be of little interest to anyone at all. Ah, well. Time will tell, as it always does.

I deprecate, however, in the strongest way the attempts which have been made lately to get at and to destroy these papers. The source of these outrages is known, and if they are repeated I have Mr. Holmes's authority for saying that the whole story concerning the politician, the lighthouse, and the trained cormorant will be given to the public. There is at least one reader who will understand.

– Dr. John H. Watson

"The Adventure of the Veiled Lodger"

Introduction: Deceptive Appearances

'Deceptive Appearances' was the first short story that I wrote that wasn't purely fan fiction.

Editor David Ruffle approached me on the GoodReads website after reading some of my BBC Sherlock fan fiction and asked if I would like to write for a new anthology of his called "Sherlock Holmes: Tales from the Stranger's Room Volume 3", to be published by MX Publishing.

I was shocked to be asked as I had never written traditional Holmes before. I decided I would set the story within the Stranger's Room of the Diogenes Club. It's not completely traditional as the idea I had would not work with Watson as the narrator.

On reading it again as I was compiling this anthology, I had a strong urge to rewrite it. I chose not to. You can see for yourself how much my writing has changed since my first venture into these waters.

This story was first published in 2017.

Deceptive Appearances

It was hard to believe that the man walking slowly towards me was the greatest mind in Britain, if not the world. The aforesaid mind was housed in a body so corpulent it was reminiscent of a pregnant hippopotamus.

He walked up to the desk I was standing at and murmured, "Is the Stranger's Room free tonight, William?"

"Yes, Mr. Holmes."

"Good. Please have a table for three set. My brother and his companion will be joining me for supper. What's available, do you know?"

"Roast beef with all the trimmings, sir. With a fine fish soup to start, bread and butter pudding for afters, and I was told to tell you that the kitchen now has that excellent French blue cheese you like to go with the port."

Mycroft Holmes fairly beamed at me. "Excellent. A fine supper for us all." He headed for the Stranger's Room, and I headed for the kitchens to let them know what was required.

I suppose I should introduce myself. My name is William Smith and I am a doorman/flunkey at the Diogenes Club. Don't bother looking it up. You won't have heard of it. It's very exclusive and very eccentric. You probably won't have heard of Mycroft Holmes either, and he would like it kept that way. You will have heard of his brother though, the great Sherlock Holmes, and his friend and biographer, Doctor John Watson. Damn them all to Hell!

The conversation flowed around the small table as I poured the port to end the meal.

"I assure you, Mycroft, my source is reliable."

"I'm sure it is, Sherlock, but, really, who would want to kill me?"

"Apart from almost everyone who knows you?"

"Holmes!" Doctor Watson, barked. "You're confusing your brother with yourself!"

Sherlock Holmes scowled at his friend, whose eyes twinkled with amusement. Mycroft Holmes chuckled richly. "Good shot, my dear doctor. A very good shot indeed."

As I poured port into the glass laid out for Mycroft, the doctor gestured with his fork, knocking the glass to the ground, spilling the fortified wine. "Oh dear…"

"It is fine, doctor. No harm is done."

"Except to the carpet."

"We've had blood on this carpet, Sherlock. A little wine isn't going to worry the cleaning staff. Any more than it worries you."

The doctor passed his glass to Mycroft. "Here. Do have mine. I haven't touched it."

Mycroft took the glass with a nod of thanks, sipping the port thoughtfully. "I understand, in theory, that certain foreign powers might want me out of the way. But at this point in time, I do not see for whom it would be advantageous to have me removed from the playing field."

"My source suggests that the Tzar of all the Russias is looking to spread his wings. You are a known peace maker, brother dear, with you out of the way there would be no-one to keep Britain and Germany from each other's throats."

"And whilst we were fighting," Doctor Watson added, "The Tzar would take the opportunity to snip a little land away from the Kaiser."

"Interesting theory." Mycroft raised his glass and studied the fluid within. "Excellent vintage, this. William?"

"Yes sir?"

"Tell the cellarman to order as many cases of this as he can. It's quite a robust little drop. Reminiscent of a good Artillery port."

"Yes sir." I turned away just as Doctor Watson managed to upset the finger bowl next to Mycroft. Water cascaded onto the floor. How did a man that clumsy get to be a doctor?

"Really, Watson, I simply cannot take you anywhere!" Sherlock Holmes openly smirked.

"Never mind, I'll just use a napkin instead of the water to clean my hands."

"Allow me, sir." I leaned over Mycroft Holmes to lay a clean napkin on his lap, I surreptitiously flexed my right wrist to release the thin bladed knife concealed there...and froze. Something cold and metallic was pressed under my right ear.

"Do not even think about it." The voice was ice cold.

The next moment I was swung away from Mycroft, my arms pinioned behind me, and handcuffs slapped around my wrists by Sherlock Holmes.

I turned my head and looked to the source of that cold voice. Doctor Watson stood there, a revolver in his hand that was pointed straight at my head. Gone was the jovial dinner companion, and the amiable buffoon. This man was more than capable of pulling the trigger and it showed in every line of his body and in the cold light in his eyes.

I was shoved into an abandoned chair.

Sherlock Holmes looked sharply at me. "It's not the Tzar who wants Mycroft dead, though, it's the Kaiser. That twaddle was for your benefit."

Mycroft Holmes smiled benignly at me. "I am curious as to why the Kaiser thought he could get away with killing me.

He hasn't anyone in his service nearly intelligent enough to outwit my brother on one of his rare off days, let alone myself." He took a meditative sip of the port and glanced at his brother.

Sherlock took up the thread again. "We knew within hours of the German government's approach to you what was happening, William, or should I say Wilhelm? Your mother is German, is she not?"

I looked away and did not reply.

Doctor Watson shook his head. "Surely you realized that all members of the Diogenes Club staff are watched?"

That was news to me. I looked quickly at Mycroft. He nodded. "With the membership including a number of politicians, wealthy businessmen, and more than a few peers, naturally security is a high priority."

Sherlock Holmes spoke again. "We kept an eye on the roster. Once we knew you would be working tonight it was child's play to organize this little charade." He smiled briefly at Doctor Watson. "My good friend is usually nowhere near as clumsy as he was tonight."

Holmes turned his attention back to me. "I know you were merely to deliver the two poisons. Your co-conspirator at the German embassy is at this moment explaining himself to the King, prior to being shipped back to Germany in ignominy. No doubt to his death, as the Kaiser cannot abide any failure, except his own. A pity, Mycroft will miss playing him at chess, and a lass in the kitchen will miss his gallant attentions. As to the your part in the matter…the sticky stem on one of the port glasses told you which glass had had poison painted in its interior, and the finger bowl with the 'X' scratched into its base told you the same poison had been spread there. The blade at your wrist was simply a contingency plan in case something went wrong."

He sipped his own port. "You're right, Mycroft. This really is an excellent port."

"I shall see that a case is delivered to Baker Street tomorrow."

Sherlock Holmes looked back to me. "It was fiendish in its simplicity. The robustness of the port would disguise any taste, and if Mycroft didn't drink the port, he would wash his fingers prior to eating the cheese, and that pungent blue cheese that he so loves would, once again, serve to disguise the taste."

The door to the Stranger's Room opened. Three burly men entered, and, at Mycroft's nod, hauled me from my seat, and out of the room.

I sit here now in a cell in the Tower of London, of all places. I haven't been tried. Mycroft advised the King against it. My 'treason' is proven by my own actions, and he doesn't want to precipitate a war between Britain and Germany. That will come. As surely as the sun will rise tomorrow, war will come.

I die today. I will be hanged by the neck, though at least my body will be given to my mother for burial. Doctor Watson assured me of this. He demanded it of Mycroft Holmes, and Mycroft consented.

I thought it was hard to believe that the greatest mind in Britain lurked in the bulk that is Mycroft Holmes. But I learned something else that night. That Doctor John H. Watson has the most deceptive appearance of all. An iron resolve and a great heart in the body of an unassuming man.

Introduction: The Mystery of the Vanishing Emeralds

This is one of two original stories for this anthology.

Back in 2020 I had dinner with two of my oldest friends here in Melbourne, whom I had met when I first moved here thirty years ago. Both Penny and David have been massively supportive of my writing. In fact, I dedicated my third novel *Sherlock Holmes and the Case of the London Dock Deaths* to them.

During dinner David told me of an idea that he had for a short story that I should write. He told me the idea, I liked it, and told him that I would write the story 'one day'.

Less than two months later, Penny rang me to tell me that David had died.

When the idea of this anthology came up, I knew that I had to write the story based on David's idea.

Dr. Andrea Williams kindly edited it for me.

I dedicate this story to the memory of David Syber, a wonderful friend who is sorely missed by all who knew him.

The Mystery of the Vanishing Emeralds

"Is there anything of interest in the newspaper this morning, my dear Watson?"

I looked up from my reading to glance at my friend who stood staring out of the window at the passing traffic on Baker Street. I looked back down at the newspaper in my hands. "Very little, I am afraid. Except for one rather odd item."

"And that is?"

"Apparently Lady Riding's emerald necklace has disappeared without trace."

Holmes turned to me; his eyebrows quirked in inquiry.

I read aloud from the paper: "At two o'clock yesterday afternoon Lady Cynthia Riding entered her bedroom to discover her jewel box open and her emerald necklace, featuring a prized emerald known as the Eye of Krishna, gone. Patrolling police constables were summoned but no trace of the necklace or the thief were to be found."

"That's not quite true," a weary voice said from the doorway.

We turned to look at our visitor.

Inspector Athelney Jones of Scotland Yard stood in our doorway. He looked both tired and frustrated in equal measures.

Holmes waved the man to a seat, which Jones accepted with apparent relief. I took a long look at the man and called Mrs. Hudson to supply tea, along with a bite of breakfast, both of which he accepted gratefully. Neither Holmes nor I spoke until Jones had finished. He sat back in his chair and gave us both a warm smile.

"Thank you, gentlemen. I have had nothing to eat since lunch yesterday."

"Shortly before you were called to Lady Riding's home?" I asked.

Athelney Jones nodded. "I was summoned to Riding House around three thirty. After the local inspector decided that it was too much for him to deal with and decided to kick the case on to Scotland Yard."

Holmes took his own seat, eyeing Jones with keen interest. "Tell me exactly what happened."

"Well, Mr. Holmes, I arrived at Riding House..."

"Which is where?"

"In Kensington. Not far from Hyde Park."

"Continue."

"The household was in an uproar, as you can imagine. Sir Phillip Riding was roaring at the servants about letting a thief into the house. Lady Cynthia was stretched out on a chaise lounge being fanned by a servant whilst her maid administered brandy."

"Were you able of ascertain how the thief gained entry?" Holmes asked.

Athelney Jones looked glum. "Through one of the many outside doors left open. Not just unlocked but standing open. It was hot yesterday, and the kitchen and scullery staff left all the doors open to try and get a little air."

"Hence Sir Phillip's rant," I said.

Jones nodded.

"So, the thief could have gained entry at any time during the day," Holmes said.

Jones nodded again.

"The thief may have been long gone before the constables were summoned," I observed.

Jones shook his head. "No. We caught the thief."

"You did?" Holmes queried. "Excellent work. So why are you here?"

"We caught the thief, but he didn't have the necklace on him. It's vanished."

"Inspector Jones, valuable emerald necklaces do not just vanish," Holmes said with some asperity.

"Maybe he had already handed it over for disposal?" I suggested.

Athelney Jones looked sour. "We went straight to Fletcher's known receivers and tore through their stocks. No sign of the necklace. We did grab two of them for possession of stolen goods, but they will probably get off." Jones's voice turned into a pleading whine "Honest. Your Honour, I bought it from a little old lady. Shabbily dressed she was, but obviously a lady. I thought she was genuine." His voice returned to its normal pitch. "Happens all the time. Maybe one in five receivers get found guilty."

"The alleged thief, Jones?"

"Fletcher. Neddy Fletcher. As grubby an individual as you ever did see. But a bloody good thief. Has the devil's own luck. Can get in and out with speed and agility. I couldn't believe my luck when two constables found him close by the house."

"But he didn't have the necklace on him," I said.

"No."

"And he denied all knowledge of the theft?" Holmes said.

"Yes."

Holmes looked at him closely. "What did you do?"

"I arrested him anyway. He's in a cell at the Yard."

"You arrested a man with no evidence that he committed a crime?"

"He had to have done it!" Athelney Jones ejaculated. "Why else would he be near the house?"

"I am fairly sure that whichever judge happens to try the case will not be impressed with that line of reasoning," Holmes said drily.

"The Superintendent isn't impressed either," Jones admitted, somewhat sourly. "I have until tomorrow afternoon to find the necklace and prove Fletcher's guilt. If I don't, Fletcher gets turned loose, and I get an official reprimand."

"And you want my help to prove Fletcher's guilt," Holmes said.

"If anyone can do it, you can, Mr. Holmes."

"Come then, let us visit Mr. Fletcher in the salubrious accommodations you have provided for him."

The cell area at Scotland Yard was quite possibly one of the most unpleasant places in London. While not obviously noxious, it was most definitely noisome. I wrinkled my nose involuntarily.

Athelney Jones chuckled. "Not what you're used to, eh, Doctor?"

"This is most unsanitary, Inspector Jones."

Jones shrugged. "Not my responsibility. Prisoners aren't kept here long. Just until they front the court."

He led us to the end of room where he stopped before a solid wooden door and flipped open the flap on it. "This is him, Mr. Holmes. Neddy Fletcher."

There was a man sitting on the bed. He was rather grubby and had his head resting in his, surprisingly clean, hands. He looked up at the sound of Inspector Jones's voice and came to the cell door. "Come to let me go, 'ave you, Inspector?" Up close the man smelled vaguely of human waste. I suspected that the jailer had not yet arranged for the slops bucket to be emptied.

Jones snorted. "You're as guilty as sin, Fletcher."

"If I stole that necklace, which I didn't, then why didn't you find it on me?" The little man's look was almost challenging. Then it became earnest.

"Here we go," Jones muttered.

"On me mother's life, I didn't nick that necklace."

Jones snorted. "Your mother died years ago, Fletcher, and if she hadn't, you'd have sold her for whatever the old duck would fetch."

Holmes raised his hand. "Enough!" He looked at Fletcher. "I have heard Inspector Jones's version of events. Now, tell me yours, Mr. Fletcher."

"'Oo the bloody 'ell are you?"

"Sherlock Holmes."

"The detective fella?" He looked over Holmes's shoulder to where I stood behind him. "And that must be the doc. Pleased to meet you, doc. Sorry I can't offer you any 'ospitality, like." Fletcher grinned at Holmes. "So old Jonesy's got you doin' 'is work for him, eh?" He chuckled humourlessly.

"Inspector Jones would like another pair of eyes to look at the evidence," Holmes replied.

"Evidence? There ain't no bloody evidence, as I didn't bloody do it!" Fletcher glared at us. "I ain't talkin' to you." He turned his back on us and walked away from the cell door.

Holmes watched Fletcher for a few moments, then turned to us, "Come, we have wasted enough time here."

"Where are we going now?" I asked.

"To visit Sir Phillip and Lady Cynthia Riding, of course."

We travelled in a police brougham to Riding House. An unctuous butler opened the door to us and, upon hearing our names, escorted us to a large study to await Sir Phillip.

Sir Phillip Riding, 6th Baronet Foxthwaite, was an impatient, overbearing, bully of a man. He stalked into the room and proceeded to attempt to intimidate my friend. Needless to say, it did not work.

"Well, Jones, where is my wife's necklace?"

"We are working on it, Sir Phillip."

Riding snorted. "Working, eh?" He looked at Holmes. "Who is this then, another incompetent johnny from the Yard." His voice was full of contempt. "Useless, the whole damn lot of you."

My friend's voice was cold. "My name is Sherlock Holmes, Sir Phillip. Inspector Jones has requested my assistance in the matter. However, if you insist on questioning my abilities, I am afraid I shall have to decline to assist."

Riding looked taken aback at being spoken to in such a manner. He grew red-faced to the point where I feared apoplexy was a distinct possibility.

"Who do you think you are?" he bellowed, spittle flecking his lips making him look rather like a rabid dog.

"I am Sherlock Holmes, as I said before." Holmes turned his head to look at me. "It seems, my dear Watson, that here is one person who has not read your charmingly inaccurate tales of my cases."

Sir Phillip continued to splutter as the door opened to admit a well-dressed woman of comparable age to Sir Phillip. She came swiftly across the room and laid a gentle hand upon his arm, before turning to my friend. "I am Lady Cynthia Riding, Mr. Holmes, it is a pleasure to meet you and a great relief to know that you are involved."

Sir Phillip looked somewhat abashed at his wife's intervention.

Holmes switched his attention from Sir Phillip to Lady Cynthia. "Can you tell me exactly what happened, Lady Cynthia, and then perhaps show me around the house?"

"Of course, Mr. Holmes," the lady replied. "We had a late lunch yesterday. Dined rather too well on Mrs. Lambert's excellent roast chicken and vegetables."

"Mrs. Lambert?" I asked.

"Our cook. She's an absolute treasure. Will not put up with nonsense from anyone." Lady Cynthia cast a sidelong glance at her husband, who I surmised had trespassed on the cook's domain once too often and got a scolding, as is the habit of good cooks everywhere. "After we had eaten, I decided to rest a while in my bedroom. When I got there, I noticed that the window beside my bed was open. It was definitely closed when I changed for lunch."

Holmes nodded approvingly at this piece of observation.

"I then looked around the room. The open window made me wonder if someone had been in my room that should not have."

"A reasonable assumption," Holmes agreed.

"Nothing had been disturbed in my drawers or my wardrobe, and I was starting to wonder if I had left the window open and forgotten about it. One does do things without thinking, and then fail to remember doing them." She paused. "Then I noticed that the lid of my jewel case was not closed properly. When I opened it, I saw that my emerald necklace had gone."

"It could not have been misplaced?" I asked.

Lady Cynthia shook her head firmly. "No. One thing I distinctly remember doing when we returned from the opera the previous night was removing the necklace myself and placing it in the box. My maid Elizabeth will confirm that."

"What opera did you attend?" Holmes asked.

Athelney Jones snorted. "What has that to do with the matter?"

"One never knows what information may be useful, Jones," my friend admonished him gently.

"We went to see La Traviata at Covent Garden. Verdi's music is so beautiful, and the singer who played Violetta had a lovely voice."

Holmes nodded. "If you could show us your room, Lady Cynthia, and then arrange for someone to show us around the rest of the property, I would be grateful."

Lady Cynthia nodded and gestured for us to follow her as she exited the room gracefully. We followed her up two sweeping flights of stairs, and along a long corridor to a large, airy, bedroom. The walls were hung with a rich green and gold wallpaper that appeared to be a William Morris design. Heavy green velvet drapes hung at the window, held open by tasselled golden cords. Outside the window the branches of an oak tree swayed in the breeze.

Holmes swept his eyes around the room, making careful note of the layout. He then crossed the room to the window, examined it carefully, opened it, examined the windowsill, and leaned out towards the tree. My friend nodded to himself, drew back into the room, and shut the window.

"I would like to speak to your maid, next, Lady Cynthia."

"Of course, Mr. Holmes."

Lady Cynthia Riding's lady's maid, Elizabeth Brown, was a short, slender, woman of mature years, with a firm no-nonsense expression. She confirmed what her mistress had said about the emerald necklace, adding that the jewel box was rarely locked as Lady Cynthia had a bad habit of misplacing the key and Sir Phillip was tired of paying for locksmiths to open it and replace the lock.

When she left us to fetch someone to take us around the property, Holmes sighed. "What do you know of the antecedents of the missing necklace, Inspector Jones?"

"Not much," the inspector replied. "Sir Phillip was a little cagey about it. I know the biggest emerald is called the Eye of Krishna, though I have no idea why."

"Probably purloined from a temple in India," I said.

Holmes nodded. "Far too many precious gems in the hands of British aristocrats have been stolen from their Eastern owners."

"Why call it the Eye of Krishna, though?" Jones asked. "Does that god have green eyes?"

"Hindus believe that those who offer emeralds to Krishna will be rewarded. The gods are believed to richly reward those who give generously," I said.

"As to the name, that was most likely given to it by the person who stole it," Holmes said.

"Aren't there curses on such gems?" Jones asked. "Could the god have taken his emeralds back?"

Holmes looked scornful. "Really, Inspector Jones, surely you don't believe such tosh?"

"The necklace has disappeared into thin air, Mr. Holmes. And maybe I'm holding a thief who really is innocent of this crime."

Holmes shook his head. "Your Neddy Fletcher is a lot of things, Inspector Jones. But innocent isn't one of them."

"Then where's the necklace?"

"All in good time, inspector."

A tall, dark-haired, young man in the livery of a footman came in. "I have been asked to show you around the house and grounds."

Holmes rubbed his chin. "I do not think we need to worry much about the house. If you could show as the gardens to the rear of the house, and the stables. I need to speak with the coachman and stable lads."

"Of course, sir. If you gentlemen would come with me?"

We followed the man back downstairs, but this time we were led to the rear of the house and through the kitchens, where the staff stopped work briefly to stare at us as our escort led us outside.

Once outside, Holmes hastened to the oak tree which we had seen from Lady Cynthia's bedroom window. He examined the tree carefully, studying the bark through his lens, and then casting around on the ground at the foot of the tree. Jones, the footman, and I stood back and watched him.

The grounds of Riding House were pleasant enough. A wrought-iron seat surrounded the trunk of the oak tree, and Holmes examined that closely as well. Directly against the wall of the house rose bushes stood in a neatly pruned line with a white painted trellis supporting them. It was a pretty, almost idyllic, scene.

After about ten minutes, Holmes returned to us and nodded to the footman. "The stables now, if you please."

"Of course, sir, this way."

We were led through a gate at the rear of the garden to a small mews. A larger building was obviously a carriage house, but closer to us were the stalls for the horses, who watched us with incurious eyes as we walked by them.

A tall, gaunt man, with skin like aged leather, approached us. "Is the master going out, Jamie?"

"No, Evans, these gentlemen are from Scotland Yard and want to talk to you."

Jamie, the footman, turned to us and said "Evans will be able to answer your questions. If you need to return to the house, just come back through the gate. Otherwise, Evans will show you the way out." Then he turned and walked away.

Evans looked at us as incuriously as the horses had. "What do you wish to speak to me about?"

"Lady Cynthia's emeralds," Holmes replied.

Evans shrugged. "First any of us knew about the theft was when the uproar started."

"Uproar?" I asked.

"The master," Evans replied. "Yelling at cook and the housemaids for leaving the doors open. Hell of a bloody ruckus."

Holmes nodded. "The night before, Sir Phillip and Lady Cynthia went to the opera at Covent Garden."

"Aye. I took them. It's not far, only about three and a half miles, but it's a bugger of a place to get in and out of. Master raises hell if I'm not there the moment they get out, so I can't bring the carriage home. Have to find a place to park and wait."

"Do you have more than one carriage?"

"Aye. Master has several, mostly at the country house. Here in town, we have two."

"Can you show me which one was used that night?"

"Aye. Come with me." With that Evans turned and walked towards the carriage house, with us following in his wake.

Inside the carriage house, Evans pointed to an elegant landau. "That's the one."

The landau was of the type known as a five-glass landau, being fitted with two windows on each side, and one at the front. Its brass lanterns positively gleamed, even in the low light of the carriage house. Holmes looked at it carefully for a moment before nodding to himself. "Thank you for showing this to us, Mr. Evans," he said. "Can you show us how to get out into the street? And then we will need to go back to the house."

"We will?" Jones asked.

"Yes. I need to speak to Miss Brown again."

Evans led the way out of the carriage house, across the mews to the rear of the stables. There, set into a wall was a wide gate. Through the bars of the gate, I could see the edge of an old stone horse trough. To the left of the gate sat a ramshackle building. I wondered for a moment if it could be a shed for the gardeners. Then the unmistakable scent of human excrement hit my nostrils. It was a privy.

Holmes turned to Evans. "It is a little unusual for a house such as this to still have an outside privy, is it not?"

"It's not for the house, sir."

"No?"

Evans shook his head. "It's for the outside workers, like myself and the lads, and the gardeners. The master don't want us trekking muck and dirt into his nice clean house."

"I see," Holmes's tone was bland.

I was beginning to develop a severe dislike of Sir Phillip Riding.

As we turned to go back to the house, Holmes said to Inspector Jones, "Where exactly did your men find Fletcher?"

Jones turned and pointed away to our right. "On the street out there. He was just coming out of the street behind these mews."

"Hmmm." Holmes looked from where Jones was pointing back to the gate, then up towards the house. Then he marched briskly back towards the house, leaving Jones and me to scurry along behind him.

Back in the house, a polite word to the housekeeper saw someone sent to fetch Miss Brown while we waited in the housekeeper's parlour.

The woman in question swept in in a swirl of skirts and indignation. "More questions? What on earth could you want now?"

"My apologies, Miss Brown," Holmes said smoothly, "but there is one thing that I need to clear up."

"And what is that?"

"What did Lady Cynthia wear to the opera that night?"

Elizabeth Brown stared at my friend as if he was completely insane. To be fair, so did Athelney Jones.

"Lady Cynthia wore an evening gown of emerald-green satin."

"Did she wear any sort of cloak?"

"No sir, it was warm enough to go without, and as they were going straight there in the landau, there was no need. Besides, Sir Phillip dislikes the delay of retrieving things from the cloak room."

"I see. Thank you, Miss Brown. You have been most helpful. If you could ask someone to show us out?"

Miss Brown gave my friend an odd look, nodded, and left the room.

Jamie the footman returned and led us to the front door. At the door, Holmes stopped and asked him "How frequently is the privy at the rear emptied?"

If the question fazed the man, he showed no sign of it. "Once a week, sir."

"When was it last emptied?"

"Three days ago, I believe."

"Have someone arrange for it to be emptied tomorrow, around ten in the morning."

"Sir Phillip will not like to pay for an extra visit, sir."

"Tell him not to worry, Scotland Yard will be paying for it."

"We will?" Inspector Jones looked startled.

Holmes glared at him.

"I mean, we will."

"And tell the men not to start clearing it until we get here. Also tell them that they will have official permission to work during the day. Oh, and Sir Phillip might like to be present as well."

With that, Holmes turned and walked into the street. We followed, and the bewildered Jamie closed the door behind us.

Athelney Jones was muttering to himself. "Evening gowns. Emptying privies. Holmes, have you gone completely mad?"

Holmes chuckled drily. "Not today. Now, my dear Inspector Jones, do make sure you are here before ten o'clock tomorrow morning. Oh, and bring Neddy Fletcher with you, there's a good chap. And do make sure that you have that permission for the night soil men to operate. Coming, Watson?" With that he walked away leaving me to hurry after him.

Jones stood beside the police brougham we had arrived in staring after my friend. "He's barking, he is," I heard Jones mumble as I hastened after Holmes.

"You know where the necklace is," I said as I caught up with Holmes.

Holmes merely smiled.

"You do. But where is it?"

Holmes's smile got a hair wider. "You know my methods, Watson. Use them."

I thought about the case all the way back to Baker Street. Once we were in our rooms, I turned to Holmes, shaking my head. "I have thought about the case, but I cannot see how you can possibly know where the emeralds are."

"The pieces of the puzzle are all there, my dear Watson. You just need to put them together."

I shook my head. "I cannot."

"Then you will just have to wait until tomorrow," Holmes replied, a trifle smugly, I thought.

We arrived at Riding House at fifteen minutes to ten o'clock. Athelney Jones arrived a few minutes later, accompanied by a handcuffed Neddy Fletcher, and two burly uniformed constables.

Holmes led the procession down beside the mews to where the gate into the gardens of Riding House stood. Fletcher was giving Holmes wary looks.

We entered the property to be met by a blustering Sir Phillip Riding. "Damn fool nonsense this. Upsetting my household…"

"Your household was upset enough by the theft," Holmes replied. "Think of this as merely setting things to rights."

Lady Cynthia, who was standing beside her husband, laid a restraining hand upon his arm. I got the feeling that reining him in was something that she had to do a lot.

"Did your man make the arrangements?" Holmes asked.

It was Lady Cynthia who replied. "Yes, Mr. Holmes. They should be here with in the next few minutes."

Fletcher gave Holmes another wary look. "Who?"

Holmes smiled at him. "The night soil men."

To my amazement, Fletcher paled so much that I feared that he might faint.

Just then the ringing of hooves on the cobbles, and the creak of a cart, heralded the arrival of the night soil men. It was unusual to see them by daylight. They were required by law to operate at night, to minimize distress to householders.

Holmes looked at Athelney Jones. "You have that permission I asked of you?"

Jones dug into his coat pocket and retrieved a letter. He handed it to Holmes. "Signed by the Superintendent and on Scotland Yard official stationery as well. Permission for the outside privy at Riding House to be cleared during daylight hours."

Four men got down from the wagon. Night soil collectors worked in teams of four. One man, known as the hole man, would enter the cess pool beneath the privy and shovel the excrement into a bucket. The second man, or rope man, would pull the full bucket up. The two tub men would then haul the bucket away to the cart. The process would continue until the cess pool was empty. It was hard, noxious work, but, perhaps unsurprisingly, it was a rather well-paid job.

The rope man approached Holmes, who took the letter from Jones and handed it to him. "Here you are, official permission to do this work in daylight."

"Thanks guvnor."

"Tell your hole man that he will most likely need a rake as well as a shovel."

The rope man looked closely at Holmes. "So that's the lie of it, is it? I'll tell him to take care."

I was more than a little bewildered by the exchange. "Holmes?" I asked.

"Hush, Watson. Let us wait. It should not be long now."

Everyone waited in silence as the night soil men commenced their work. It was no more than fifteen minutes later when the hole man let out a shout. The cess pool muffled his words, but the tone was one of excitement.

The rope man looked across at us. "Can we get a bucket of water?"

A curious crowd of Riding's workers had gathered to watch what was happening. Evans, the coachman we had spoken with the previous day, nudged a stable lad, who hurried away and came back with a bucket of water which he carefully carried up to the privy.

The hole man emerged from the cess pool and dropped what appeared to be a large lump of excrement into the bucket. He and the bucket men watched as the rope man swirled the bucket around, then plucked a rag from his pocket and plunged it into the water, clearly scrubbing something.

After a couple of minutes, the rope man straightened up with a grin, and withdraw his hands from the bucket. He came towards us bearing something wrapped in the now sodden rag.

He grinned at Holmes. "Was this what yer had us looking for, guv?"

The rag was unfolded to reveal a glint of gold and a flash of green fire.

Lady Cynthia clasped a hand to her throat. "My emeralds!"

Neddy Fisher looked vaguely ill. "You can't prove I put them there!"

Holmes turned to him, then looked at Athelney Jones. "I take it Mr. Fletcher here is still in the clothes he wore that day?"

"He is," Jones confirmed. Then with a flash of humour he said, "Scotland Yard isn't the Dorchester, Mr. Holmes. No hot baths or room service."

Holmes turned back to Fletcher. "I can prove without a shadow of a doubt that you were on the premises. You left imprints of your boots in the soil in the shade of the oak tree, and a fine muddy boot mark on the seat surrounding the tree. Combined with your presence in a place you had no business being, not to mention your history of theft..."

"That's enough to send you down for a nice long stretch," Athelney Jones cut in. "Be thankful they no longer hang for theft, Neddy lad."

Fletcher's shoulders dropped. "How did you know where I hid them?"

"I would quite like to know that too," I said.

"As would I," Jones said.

"Then come to Baker Street this evening, Jones, and I shall tell you both then."

Sir Phillip Riding came forth and shook my friend's hand vigorously. "Damn fine work, sir. Damn fine indeed. You have my thanks."

"You are most welcome, Sir Phillip, Lady Cynthia." Holmes turned to me. "Come, my friend, we have taken up enough of these people's time." He turned back to Sir Phillip and Lady Cynthia. "I wish you both a pleasant day." With that he walked away. I said my goodbyes to the Ridings and Athelney Jones and followed him.

Out of the street, Holmes turned to me, "Well, that was a pleasant morning's work. What do you say to a little lunch at Simpson's?"

"Capital idea, Holmes," I replied.

Athelney Jones arrived at 7 o'clock that evening. I poured him a brandy as he took the seat Holmes waved him too.

"The Superintendent sends his congratulations, Mr. Holmes. And you have mine as well. You saved my bacon well and truly."

Holmes waved a languid hand. "I am sure you would have worked it out eventually, Jones."

"Perhaps," the man admitted, "…but most likely not. That was a fair old piece of detective work, make no mistake."

"Indeed, it was," I said, taking my seat. "And you did say you would tell us how you worked it out."

"When did you know that Fletcher was the thief?" I asked.

"I knew that as soon as I saw him in the cell."

"But how? There was nothing to see in the cell."

Holmes chuckled. "As always, my dear Watson, you see but you do not observe. You saw a man in a cell. I observed a man in a cell with hands that were too clean, an empty slops bucket, and the lingering odour of excrement. The rest fell into place when we visited Riding House."

Holmes took a meditative sip of his brandy before continuing. "Once I had spoken with Lady Cynthia, her maid, the coachman, and the footman, I then knew the sequence of events and where the emeralds were."

Athelney Jones placed his brandy on the table and leaned forward. "Tell us exactly what happened, Mr. Holmes. I'm blowed if I can tell how you worked it out."

Holmes sat back in his chair. "It all started with the opera."

"The opera?" Jones looked bewildered.

"Your Neddy Fletcher was in Covent Garden. It is notorious for thieves and pickpockets as you well know. Exactly where he was is immaterial, but he saw Sir Phillip and Lady Cynthia leaving the opera house. Dressed in vivid green satin, and with the emeralds around her neck, Lady Cynthia stood out, as was her intention. It was not, however, her intention to catch the eye of a known thief. The landau with its bright brass lanterns made it easy to follow."

"All the way from Covent Garden to Kensington?" I objected.

"It is a matter of a mere three and a half miles," Holmes replied. "Not to mention the fact that those of Sir Phillip's ilk almost all have their townhouses in and around Kensington. The roads would have been fairly crowded. It would not have been difficult for an active man such as Neddy Fletcher to keep up with the coach. He probably rode part of the way perched on the back of a less opulent carriage."

I nodded my understanding.

"So, Fletcher followed the Ridings home," Jones said.

Holmes nodded. "Once he had identified the house, he then went down behind the mews to locate a place to enter."

"How would he know which room was Lady Cynthia's?" I asked.

"At that time of night, there would be very few windows alight. Most of the servants would have retired for the night. It was simply a process of elimination. Moreover, he may well have seen Lady Cynthia's shadow moving against the drapes."

I once again nodded my understanding.

"The next day, Fletcher returned to carry out the theft, entering through the gate into the alley behind the mews. He stood for a while in the shadows beneath the oak tree. Either to wait for someone to move out of sight, or to judge the easiest way to climb the tree and reach Lady Cynthia's bedroom."

"He climbed the tree?" Jones looked startled.

"Of course, he climbed the tree. The tree had broken twigs and scuffed bark that made it obvious someone had climbed it recently. How did you think he got in, Jones?"

"I thought he just walked in."

Holmes snorted. "He would have been caught before he got clear of the kitchens. Too many people coming and going."

"The open doors…" Jones said feebly.

"Were just that. Doors left open to catch some hint of breeze. Fletcher climbed the tree and opened the window which clearly had not been locked."

"How do you know that?" I asked.

"There was no sign of damage to either the lock or the window frame," Holmes replied. "Fletcher climbed into the room, took the necklace from the unlocked jewel box and proceeded to climb back out of the window. He did not get clear though. Fletcher was certainly still close to the building when Lady Cynthia entered the room to find her necklace gone.

Her screams would have alerted him. Fletcher, however, did not panic."

"What did he do?" I asked.

"He slipped across the garden and into the privy, where he dropped the necklace into the cess pool. When it did not sink far enough, he had to use his hands to push it below the surface."

My nose wrinkled involuntarily at the idea of putting my hands into a cess pool. Holmes noticed my expression and gave a wintry smile. "An unappealing prospect, I agree, my dear Watson. Fletcher then slipped out into the alley, pausing to scrub his hands as clean as possible in the horse trough. He hid in the shadows of the alley for a good long while before he sauntered away but had the misfortune of walking into the arms of the constabulary."

Jones was frowning. "But how did you know where Fletcher had hidden the emeralds?"

"When we accompanied you to see Fletcher at Scotland Yard, I was struck by three things."

"And they were?" Jones asked.

"As I said just before: Fletcher's clean hands, the empty slops bucket, and the lingering smell of excrement."

Jones and I exchanged puzzled looks.

Holmes sighed at our confusion. "The slops bucket being empty told me there was no reason for the smell. Therefore, the smell had to come from another source. Once I saw where the outside privy was located at Riding House, the reason for the smell, and the clean hands, became clear."

"Astounding," I cried.

"Elementary," Holmes responded.

Athelney Jones got to his feet. "Be that as it may, I thank you for solving this case." He smiled mischievously. "If the good doctor writes about this case, he will have a hard time coming up with an acceptable title."

I laughed. "How does 'The Mystery of the Vanishing Emeralds' sound, inspector?"

Jones laughed again. "I look forward to reading it. Good night, gentlemen."

Introduction: Best Served Cold

Back in May 2020 during a conversation on Twitter with Margie Deck that was loaded with extremely bad (but funny) baking puns, the idea was raised to do an anthology focused on Sherlock Holmes and baking. The idea was tossed around, then shelved, then in August it flamed into life as *Sherlock Holmes of Baking Street.*

'Best Served Cold' was my contribution to the anthology, which was edited by Margie Deck and Nancy Holder and published by Belanger Books in 2021.

Best Served Cold

The young lady who sat in our sitting room was the model of decorum and control, except for the anxious manner in which she twisted a handkerchief between her hands.

"It is the man I am to marry, Mr. Holmes. James Martin," she said. "We were going to announce our engagement at my birthday dinner on Saturday."

The past tense caught my friend's ear. "You were going to announce it?" Holmes asked.

The young lady, Miss Violet Creighton, nodded. "James has disappeared. Gone, without a word to anyone. It isn't like him, Mr. Holmes. It truly isn't. James is thoughtful and caring."

The older man who had accompanied her, and who had introduced himself as her uncle, Alfred Creighton, patted her hand before turning to speak to us. "My niece is correct, gentlemen. James is intelligent and thoughtful, as well as hard working, which is why I gave my consent to the marriage. James was a childhood friend of Violet's."

Violet gave us a distressed look. "James would not disappear without warning. I went to his lodgings, but the harridan who runs them would not let me in. Nor would she allow Jack to enter."

"Jack?" I asked.

"Jack Kincaid," Alfred Creighton replied. "Jack was also a childhood friend of Violet and James. Works as hard as James. He is a baker. He owns a little bakery on Marylebone High Street. Quite close to James's lodgings, in fact."

Holmes obtained Mr. Martin's address from them, as well as their own, before nodding briskly and saying, "I shall call upon you once I have something substantive to tell you."

I showed Mr. Creighton and his niece to the door, before returning to Holmes.

"You think there is something odd about this young man's disappearance?" I asked. It was unlike my friend to take up so slender a thread to investigate.

As usual, my friend followed my train of thought. Holmes shrugged. "We will most likely find that the young man has had cold feet and, not being able to cope with the scene that would most likely ensue, has quietly disappeared of his own accord"

"He would not be the first young man to do that," I commented.

"Indeed. However, I would have expected in that case for some sort of letter or note to have been sent to the young lady. The fact that none has lends an element of uncertainty to the situation." Holmes consulted his pocket watch. "Mr. Martin lives in rooms not far from here. We have time to visit them before lunch. We shall collect Lestrade from Scotland Yard first, I think."

"Lestrade?"

"The landlady would not let Miss Creighton into Mr. Martin's rooms, and rightly so. Such a stalwart individual would most likely not allow us in either, but an inspector from Scotland Yard is a different kettle of fish entirely."

This proved to be the case. Lestrade came with us willingly enough. Commenting that he would rather solve a missing person case than a murder.

The lady in question did indeed object to our wishing to inspect James Martin's rooms, but as Holmes had suggested, she caved entirely to Lestrade's authority.

An inspection of the rooms proved interesting in that nothing was missing at all. It was as if James Martin had walked out of his rooms and simply disappeared.

Back out on the street, I looked at Holmes. "What now?"

Holmes gestured down the street towards a bakery. "Now we have a word with Mr. Kincaid."

"Kincaid?" Lestrade asked.

"Local baker and childhood friend of both the missing man and Miss Creighton," I replied.

The bakery was busy when we entered. It appeared to be doing excellent business. The savoury smells of meat pies and pasties filled the air. A sign above the counter proclaimed that the bakery's speciality was pork pies, and, indeed, there was a fine selection of pork pies on display.

A strong-shouldered, brawny chap, more like a butcher than a baker, approached us. "Good morning, gentleman, what can I get you this fine day?"

"Are you Mr. Jack Kincaid?" Holmes asked.

"I am indeed. May I ask who you gentlemen would be?"

"I am Sherlock Holmes, this gentleman is Doctor John Watson, and the fellow next to him is Inspector Lestrade of Scotland Yard."

"And what can I do for three such notable gentlemen?" Kincaid asked, eyebrows arched in query.

"James Martin is missing, as you are aware. His fiancée, Miss Creighton is extremely worried."

Jack Kincaid shrugged his massive shoulders. "Violet came to me bleating something about Jimmy being missing. I tried to enquire at his rooms." He paused. "I take it you have been to his rooms?"

"We have," said Lestrade.

"Then you will have met the gorgon who guards the gates. I couldn't get through the door. Besides which, I doubt he's gone far. Probably gone away to get some peace from Miss Bossy-Britches."

"Mr. Martin did not confide in you?" Holmes asked. "I was under the impression that you were friends."

Kincaid shook his head in denial. "We were friends. Once. When we were children. But we grew up. Violet's parents died and she went to live with her rich uncle, who has settled quite a sum on her that she will get when she turns twenty-five, which is on Saturday. Jimmy moved away to live with his grandfather and then went to work for a bank." The baker's tone turned bitter. "Neither of them had time for me. I may own a bakery, started by my grandfather, but to both their minds I work with my hands, and therefore, am not as good as they are. Which is quite amusing if you consider that when we were children I was the most affluent of the trio."

None of us quite knew how to respond to that confession, but Mr. Kincaid did not appear to be concerned by our lack of response. He disappeared back behind the counter and returned with a cloth wrapped bundle, which he opened to display several delicious looking pork pies. The cloth was folded back over them, and he handed them to my friend. "On the house, Mr. Holmes. Sorry you had to come here for nothing."

We stopped at Baker Street long enough to give the pork pies to Mrs. Hudson, who greeted them with pleasure. She was already planning a meal based around them as we left.

From Baker Street we went to the house of Mr. Creighton. He was most disturbed to learn that James Martin had apparently disappeared without trace. My friend assured him that we would continue to look for him and Lestrade said he would make enquiries at the local police station. As we sat talking in Mr. Creighton's study, we could hear a distant commotion in the house. Alfred Creighton sent for his niece, who arrived pink-cheeked and smiling. "Jack Kincaid has sent a gift of pork pies for Saturday night,"

My friend' eyes narrowed. "A strange gift," he commented. "Miss Creighton, may I prevail upon you for some samples of the pies?"

"Of course, Mr. Holmes." The young lady could see nothing out of the ordinary in my friend's request, but her uncle gave him a sharp look.

Miss Creighton went to the kitchen and returned with several pies wrapped in a cloth, which Holmes took from her carefully. She returned to the kitchen, and we took our leave. Holmes said nothing to Mr. Creighton until we reached the door, whereupon he advised the man not to allow anyone in the household to consume the pies.

Alfred Creighton assured him that he would give the order, but as the pies had been sent for Violet's birthday, no-one would be likely to eat one before the coming Saturday.

Outside Lestrade spoke up, "You suspect poison?"

Holmes frowned. "Perhaps. In any case I find it strange that a man who was as bitter as Mr. Kincaid was when speaking to us, would take it upon himself to act in such a manner. It is unusual and, I think, needs to be investigated."

Lestrade nodded. "Give me one of the pies, will you? I will get the police surgeon to do a Marsh Test on it. Arsenic is the most likely poison, after all."

Holmes nodded and unwrapped the bundle and handed a pork pie to Lestrade. We said our farewells and went on our separate ways.

As soon as we had returned to Baker Street, Holmes went to Mrs. Hudson and obtained one of the pork pies he had given her. He then began to set up his various items of chemistry equipment. I realized that I would be in the way, so took myself out of the flat in search of lunch and a pleasant afternoon at my club.

Returning the Baker Street several hours later, I spied Wiggins leaving the house carrying a small bundle, which I assumed contained pork pies.

When I reached our rooms, several of the pork pies that had been obtained from the Creighton's sat upon the table. The lunch at my club had been indifferent and the pies looked succulent. The hot water pastry was baked a deep golden brown. I felt it was unlikely that Holmes would leave the pies sitting on the table if they were poisoned, so I picked one up. I sniffed at it gently, savouring its meaty, spicy aroma.

As I opened my mouth to take a bite, the pie was dashed from my hand. Holmes stood beside me, his face white and pinched. "For the love of God, Watson! Do not eat that!" I looked at him, then at the pie now laying on the floor, and then back at Holmes.

"I did not think you would leave poisoned pies on the table," I explained lamely.

The look Holmes gave me was terrible. "There is no poison in the pies, Watson. I fear it is much worse than that."

He refused to explain further, wrapping up the remaining pies and stowing them away in his room, away from all temptation. "If you fancy a pork pie, my good Watson, I suggest you get one of the ones Kincaid gave us himself. Those contain nothing more than the flesh of good Berkshire pigs."

I found, however, that I had lost my appetite for a pork pie. The look on Holmes's face had been dreadful.

Wiggins was back before dark with a message for Holmes. "The old man says to tell yer that yer right in yer suspicions. The second pie contains what yer thought it did." The lad paused. "'E didn't eat much of it. Took a bite an' spat it back out. Waste o' good food, that is."

Holmes digested the message in silence, gave Wiggins some coins and sent him on his way.

I looked at my friend. "What now?" I asked softly. The message meant nothing to me, but Holmes's face had pinched tight again.

"Now? Now, Watson we summon Lestrade and arrest a murderer."

Jack Kincaid was dragged to the police wagon by several large constables. Holmes and I stood slightly up the street watching the proceedings.

A rather green looking Lestrade exited the bakery and came towards us. "You were right, Holmes. We found the skull hidden beneath a floorboard in the scullery. I suspect the rest of the skeleton is mixed in with the usual pig bones to be collected by the rag and bone man. I'm sending the barrel of bones to the police surgeon for sorting."

"It is definitely James Martin?" I asked. "All we really have is a skull."

"It's Martin, all right," said Lestrade. "We found Martin's watch and chain hidden, macabrely enough, inside Martin's skull. The watch is engraved with Martin's initials and there is a small lock of hair in the back of it. The colour is certainly consistent with Miss Creighton's. Besides which, one of the lads that works in the bakery told us that Kincaid had sent him up to Petticoat Lane to sell a fine suit of gent's clothes. When the lad asked where the clothes had come from Kincaid told him they'd been giving as payment to settle an account."

"It would not be the first time that has happened," I commented.

Lestrade nodded, "Except for the fact that the lad recognized the waistcoat as belonging to James Martin. He'd seen him wearing it. The lad is also a little less than honest."

"He stole the waistcoat," Holmes said.

"That he did. I should give him a lecture about theft and where it leads, except that the boy has done us an enormous favour. More evidence to use to hang Kincaid."

"I doubt he will hang," Holmes said softly. "His most likely destination is one of the asylums. Most probably Broadmoor."

Lestrade watched as the police wagon was driven away. "I would like to say that I think you are wrong, Mr. Holmes. But I am all too afraid that you are right." He looked back at my friend. "How on earth did you work out that Kincaid had murdered Martin and made him into pork pies?"

"You heard how bitter Kincaid was about James Martin and Violet Creighton," Holmes replied. "There was no reason for him to be so generous as to make a gift of pork pies to Miss Creighton for her birthday. Leaving aside the fact that pork pies are a strange gift to give at any time. You both know my adage that when you have eliminated the impossible, whatever remains, *however improbable, must be the truth.*"

Both Lestrade and I nodded silently.

"I tested those pies for every poison I could think of, with no result. When I compared one of the pies given to Miss Creighton with the ones given to us, I noticed that the colour and the texture of the filling were slightly different. So I sent one of each pie to an expert."

"An expert?" asked Lestrade.

"There is an old man I know," Holmes said softly, "who went to sea as a cabin boy when he was just a lad. The ship he was on was wrecked in the South Seas. He and some others made it to a small island. The natives were less than friendly.

For some reason, perhaps his age, the chief took a shine to the lad and let him live, adopting him into the tribe. His shipmates were not so fortunate."

"They ate them?" Lestrade looked faintly sick.

"Some places refer to human flesh as 'long pig'," I said as realization dawned.

"Just so, Watson. I am told that once tasted it is never forgotten. And according to Wiggins, a small taste was all the old man needed to take before he could confirm my hypothesis."

"But why?" I asked. "Why would Kincaid do such a thing? It is an extreme reaction to broken friendships."

"I suspect, my friend, that though he has not said it, Jack Kincaid wished to marry Miss Creighton himself."

"But she would not look at him in that light, because he is in trade," I said.

"Exactly," said Holmes.

"So he set out for revenge, said Lestrade, shaking his head.

"Indeed," said Holmes. "Revenge, like a pork pie, is best served cold."

Introduction: The Rubies of Bast

This is the second of the original stories for this anthology.

I ran a little contest on my Facebook page asking people to give me word prompts. The winner to receive an autographed copy of this anthology. I ran the entries through a Random Number Generator to find the winner.

The winner was Angela Poppleton with her prompt of "Tourist/Scarab/Bast/Rubies".

The story naturally leant itself to involving the British Museum's Egyptology department. As the novel I am working on also involves that department I decided to use a character I had already created for *Sherlock Holmes and the Curse of Neb-Heka-Ra,* rather than create a new one. So, you get to meet Mr. Henry Cavanagh here. He is going to have a rather important role in the novel, and I have become rather fond of him.

The story has been edited by Dr. Andrea Williams.

The Rubies of Bast

It was a warm afternoon in early September when Mr. Henry Cavanagh came to Baker Street to consult my old friend, Mr. Sherlock Holmes.

We had met Cavanagh a year or two previously during a case that became known as *The Curse of Neb-Heka-Ra*. Henry Cavanagh was a curator in the Ancient Egypt department at the British Museum. He was a tall man with dark, curly hair, and warm, brown eyes whose usual expression of lively curiosity had been replaced with one of concern and worry.

My friend showed Cavanagh to a chair, his own face showing his curiosity at the man's unannounced visit.

Cavanagh got quickly to the point. "I need your help, Mr. Holmes."

I handed the man a medicinal tot of brandy. He thanked me with his eyes and took a sip.

"What has happened?" Holmes asked.

"The British Museum is assisting at a private exhibition run by one of the directors of the museum, Herbert Wallingford, who, amongst his other hobbies, actually goes on digs in Egypt. Two years ago, his team found the ruins of a temple of the goddess Bast, or Bastet, close by what was the ancient city of Bubastis. The city was the centre of the worship of the goddess, and the first pharaoh of the 22nd Dynasty, Shoshenq I, had a royal residence there. The team believe that the temple they found was Shoshenq's private one, rather than the main temple complex."

"They believe?" asked Holmes.

Cavanagh shrugged. "It is a possibility. There is no proof. There are inscriptions with Shoshenq's name, but no dedication as such. Wherever there was a royal residence you will find royal names. But they did find a number of interesting artifacts. Statues of the pharaoh, of his family, his courtiers, and of the goddess herself. They also found something unique."

"And that was?" I asked.

"A complete pectoral, or breast plate. Usually they are found broken, but this one is whole, and of an interesting pattern. The centre piece is a large scarab beetle carved from carnelian, supported by two Bast cats carved from onyx. The whole thing is strung on gold wire with alternating blue and green faience beads. It is both gaudy and beautiful beyond words. When the sun hits it, it simply lights up with a fiery radiance. So much so that the team named it 'The Rubies of Bast'."

"Something has happened to this pectoral," Holmes stated.

Cavanagh looked at him in surprise. "It has. How did you know?"

Holmes smiled briefly. "You would not make such a point of telling us about it, if it was not central to the reason for your visit."

"Correct." Cavanagh's smile was equally brief. "The exhibition is being held, not at the museum, but in rooms in Montague Street. The museum was happy to supply assistance but did not want to have it under our roof because of Wallingford's insistence on billing it as the 'Treasures of Shoshenq's Private Temple'. It made the other directors cross because, as I said, there is no proof, so supporting it as a private exhibition was a compromise."

"Understandable," I commented.

"The exhibition has been running for about eight days without any trouble. Then this afternoon disaster struck."

"What happened?" Holmes asked softly.

"A family came into the exhibition. Nothing special about them. They had a bit of money, probably from trade."

"How do you know?" Holmes asked.

"All three were well dressed, the woman was wearing a fine ruby brooch pinned to her left breast, but their accents were Northern. But not Northern aristocracy or even landed gentry," Cavanagh replied.

Holmes nodded his approval of Cavanagh's observation and gestured for him to continue.

"They had been there about fifteen minutes when the woman began to scream that someone had stolen her brooch."

"From right off her breast?" I said, thinking it highly unlikely. "Surely the catch came loose, and it fell?"

Cavanagh nodded. "That is what we thought, so we closed the doors and began to search the rooms. There was no sign of the brooch. Then we realised something."

"And that was?" Holmes asked.

"The pectoral was also missing!"

Holmes fairly beamed at the man. "My dear Cavanagh, you do bring me an interesting puzzle. I assume you sent for the police?"

Cavanagh nodded. "I sent one of the guards to Scotland Yard. I told him to insist on Inspector Lestrade being sent."

"Excellent. You have a carriage downstairs?"

"I do."

"Then Watson and I shall accompany you back and wait for Lestrade to arrive before we begin."

When we went downstairs, I saw Wiggins across the road. Holmes saw him as well, and titled his head towards the coach we were to be travelling in.

As it turned out, Lestrade beat us to the building housing the exhibition and was waiting for us on the footpath in Montague Street. Two uniformed constables stood nearby. Lestrade greeted us cordially, before turning to Cavanagh. "Your man told me a pretty tale of disappearing rubies and ancient artifacts. He made it sound like some mysterious Egyptian deity took a liking to a visitor's jewellery and took off with it."

Cavanagh winced. "I knew I should not have sent Wilson. He is a bit of a romantic. But he was spouting off about the goddess reclaiming her own. I felt I needed to get him out from underfoot."

"Before someone sent him to Colney Hatch?" I asked.

"I nearly did myself," Lestrade said. "Only I knew you would not have sent a madman to me without a good reason, Cavanagh."

"He isn't mad," Cavanagh said. "Just a romantic."

I am not completely sure, but I thought I heard Holmes mutter "It is much the same thing."

Cavanagh led the way into a fine Georgian terrace house. A discreet sign by the window advised that inside was a display of treasures from the private temple of Sheshonq I. Entry times and costs were written at the bottom of the sign. I almost choked at the entry fee. This was not an exhibition for the average man. The entry cost was a sovereign. A hellishly expensive fee for an exhibition of any sort. Clearly Herbert Wallingford did not want any riffraff visiting. The cost however, had obviously not deterred whomever it was who had stolen both brooch and breast plate.

We could hear a woman complaining in a loud voice, with a very strong Yorkshire accent, as we entered the building. Holmes looked at Cavanagh. The man winced. "Mrs. Crowther," he explained. "The owner of the brooch."

Holmes nodded and we continued up the stairs. Cavanagh led us into a large room where the walls were lined with glass-fronted cases that contained objects that were obviously from the excavation. Just inside the doorway stood two matching statues of cats, carved from some sort of black stone. They stood about four feet high, all four paws together, and bodies erect. They stared into the room with a stare that was almost judgmental. An empty display case sat prominently in the middle of the room. This, obviously, was the case that had contained the mysteriously missing pectoral.

A plump woman of matronly appearance was leaning against the shoulder of a hard-faced man, who, from the way he was holding her and patting her shoulder was clearly her husband. This was obviously the owner of the missing brooch. I noticed that the hand that the man had resting on his wife's shoulder was deformed. The middle finger was bent and twisted. It looked like an old injury, quite possibly a break that had not healed well.

The hard-faced man looked at us as we entered the room. His eyes flicked from myself, to Holmes, and then to Lestrade. He shifted his gaze to Cavanagh. "Who are these men?" he demanded.

Cavanagh gestured to us. "Three men that I am confident will be able to help. Inspector Lestrade of Scotland Yard, and Mr. Sherlock Holmes and Doctor Watson. I believe you may have heard of them."

The words *even in Yorkshire* went unspoken. An odd expression flitted briefly across the man's face. "Aye, I've heard of you all."

Cavanagh turned to us, "Gentlemen, this is Mr. Barnaby Crowther and his wife. Standing against the wall and in front of the other door there are guards that are usually in the employ of the British Museum: Stanley Wilson, whom you have met, Inspector; Robert James, Simon Steale, and John Campsey."

The four men, clad in identical uniforms of black serge, nodded their heads to us.

"I should like to examine the premises before we speak to anyone, Cavanagh," Holmes said.

"Of course," Cavanagh replied.

Holmes made straight for the empty display case. He removed his magnifying lens from his pocket and began to examine the case.

"Ain't no point in lookin' at that, Mr. 'Olmes," one of the guards said. "The goddess came an' took back 'er necklace."

"I do not think so, Mr. Wilson," Holmes replied, not looking up from his examination. "I rather feel that goddesses would not need to pick locks. And this lock has quite clearly been picked."

Holmes handed his lens to Lestrade who looked at the lock, and then handed the lens to me. Viewing the lock through the lens the minute scratches around the lock were clear. Someone had most definitely picked the lock.

The guard was staring open-mouthed at Holmes. "Blimey! 'Ow did 'e know me name?"

The void of embarrassment was filled by the entrance of a small black cat. The feline wandered up to my friend and proceeded to weave her way around his ankles. Holmes looked down, startled, then gave a slight smile and bent down to scratch behind the animal's ears.

"That is Bast," Cavanagh said. "A stray. She wandered in on the first day and refused to leave."

Lestrade eyed the cat. "Looks pretty well fed for a stray."

Cavanagh and the guards looked embarrassed. Wilson piped up with "I gives 'er some o' the meat from my sandwiches."

Another guard, Campsey, muttered something about his father being a fishmonger and there were plenty of scraps going free.

"Of course," Cavanagh said. "We do make sure there is a bowl of water for her outside."

"Not to mention the cream that mysteriously appears when you do, sir," said Steale, with a perfectly straight face.

It was obvious that the animal had fallen quite firmly on her paws and would no doubt either relocate to the museum or one of the guard's homes when the exhibition was over.

"Damn the animal," snarled Barnaby Crowther.

"Not a fond of cats, sir?" asked Lestrade.

"Filthy animals," the man snapped. "Shouldn't be inside."

Holmes looked at the man. "What is it that you do, Mr. Crowther?"

"I am a merchant. I deal in grain. Corn, millet, wheat, barley and the like."

"I see." Holmes gave the cat another scratch before straightening up and turning his attention to the man.

The cat leapt up onto the empty display case, gave herself a perfunctory wash, before setting herself to watch the proceedings. Her posture made me think of the cat statues beside the door.

"Now, Mr. Crowther, about this brooch…"

Mrs. Crowther let out a wail. "It was ruby, it was. It was a gift from my dear husband, and now it's gorn."

Barnaby Crowther gave his wife a sharp look. "Do be quiet, Lizzie. Man can't hear himself think." He turned back to my friend. "As my wife said, the brooch was a gift from me. A cabochon ruby in a gold setting. I bought it for her about three years ago. I know it's not the sort of thing one wears during the day, but my wife felt it would be appropriate to wear it when coming to view the Rubies of Bast."

Cavanagh sighed. "Carnelian."

"Pardon?"

"The gem on the pectoral is a large carnelian. As I told Mr. Holmes and Doctor Watson earlier, it was the archaeological team that named the pectoral the Rubies of Bast. Because of the way it flames when the light hits it."

"And, no doubt, because the Rubies of Bast will draw more of a crowd than the Carnelians of Bast," Holmes added dryly.

"That as well," Cavanagh agreed.

Crowther looked astonished. Mrs. Crowther looked shocked. Turning her eyes in mute appeal to her husband, but I did not understand the message. Holmes caught the look and nodded to himself. Obviously, my friend understood what was going on.

Lestrade looked around the room. "Is everyone still here that was present when the thefts were discovered?"

"Everyone else is in the other room," Cavanagh replied, gesturing towards the door at the rear of the room. Now I understood why the guards were standing there. To prevent anyone from leaving.

One of the guards cleared his throat. "Not everyone, Mr. Cavanagh, sir."

Cavanagh turned to him. "What do you mean, James?"

The guard, Robert James, scratched his head. "Well, sir, I noticed when we were guiding people in that the lad that was with these people," he gestured towards Mr. and Mrs. Crowther, "…was missing."

"You did not think to mention this before?" Lestrade asked.

James shrugged. "Didn't get a chance to, Inspector."

"Missing?" Mrs. Crowther's voice rose into an ear-piercing wail. "My son! My Barty! Someone stole him as well!"

Lestrade closed his eyes as a pained expression crossed his face.

Barnaby Crowther snapped at his wife. "Shut up, woman! Let the men think."

"But Barty…"

"Our Bartholomew will be all right. He probably just ran away when the fuss started."

"But he's all alone. Lost in London. This is a bad place! Things happen…"

"Things happen at home as well. Now be quiet, woman!" Barnaby Crowther's voice held an edge that I did not like. I suspected that if we had not been present, he would have hit his wife. Mrs. Crowther seemed to think so as well, because she subsided into a meek bundle huddled on the chair.

A look of intense dislike flashed across the faces of both Lestrade and Cavanagh. Holmes, as always, remained inscrutable.

"We shall look for the boy as well as the brooch," Lestrade said. "How old is Bartholomew?"

"The lad's fourteen, Inspector. We brought him with us to see the exhibition and to see London. He's following me into the business. He needs to see how everything works, and that involves visiting the capital," Crowther replied.

"Where in Yorkshire are you from?" Holmes asked.

"Bradford," the man replied.

"Good textile area," Holmes observed. "Woollen cloth, I believe."

"Yes, indeed. And all those workers need to eat, which is why I do so well selling grain."

Holmes nodded and stepped back from the conversation. I saw him slip down the stairs. I followed him in time to see him slip some coins to one of his Baker Street Irregulars. The lad turned away and I saw it was Wiggins. I realized that Holmes's head tilt had been to tell Wiggins to follow us.

It occurred to me that Wiggins must now be around the same age as the missing Bartholomew Crowther.

Holmes smiled briefly when he saw me, and we went back into the room.

Mr. Crowther was explaining to Lestrade about the disappearing brooch. "We had just finished looking at the Rubies of Bast. A fine piece, even if they aren't real rubies. As we turned away from the case, my wife put her hand to her breast and realized that the brooch was gone."

"I see," said Lestrade, as he made notes in him notebook. He folded it up and tucked it in his coat pocket. "Where are you staying?"

"The Northumberland Hotel."

"Well, Mr. Crowther, perhaps you and your wife would like to return there…"

"With suitable police accompaniment, Lestrade," Holmes interjected smoothly. "I am sure they will find the presence of a couple of uniformed constables comforting."

Lestrade shot my friend a sharp look. "Of course, my two constables will remain…"

"Inside the room, don't you think?" said Holmes. "After all, we do not want to give other guests at the hotel the wrong impression."

"Inside the room, of course," Lestrade said. "As you say, Holmes, we do not want to give the other guests the wrong impression."

"I'm sure that's not necessary," said Mr. Crowther.

Lestrade looked at him. "It most definitely is. You are a distinguished visitor to this city. We must do our best for you."

We waited in silence as Mr. and Mrs. Crowther were escorted out by the two constables. Neither of them protested again, to be honest, they seemed stunned by what was happening. I will own that I myself was most perplexed by the proceedings.

It was not until the door closed downstairs that Lestrade turned to my friend and said, "What on earth was that about?" His voice held a note of anger.

Holmes was unperturbed. "The Crowthers are the most likely thieves. They were closest to the case when the pectoral was discovered gone."

"But Mrs. Crowther's brooch was stolen!" Wilson said.

"Was it? We only have her word that it was."

"She was wearing it. I saw it!" Wilson objected.

"I never said that she was not wearing it," Holmes replied. "Only that she alone says it was stolen."

Lestrade nodded thoughtfully. "I have seen some sharp pickpockets in my time, but never one that good. Not even Dickybird Sikes."

"Dickybird?" I asked.

"Richard Sikes. Known as Dickybird to his intimates. Young lad he was when I last saw him. He is the illegitimate grandson of the notorious thief William 'Bill' Sikes. He came out of jail about three years ago and promptly disappeared."

Holmes raised his eyebrows. "You never thought to wonder where he went?"

Lestrade shrugged. "As long as he is not in London, he is not my problem. Lord knows I have enough problems without adding overly clever pickpockets to the list."

Holmes nodded.

"What do we do now?" I asked.

Holmes looked at Cavanagh. "Have the other visitors been spoken with?"

"Yes, Mr. Holmes," Cavanagh replied. "They were all quite shocked at the theft. Every one of them either turned out either their pockets or their purses. We only asked them to remain in case you wished to speak with them."

"Excellent," Holmes said. "Then I think we should have a brief word with them and then let them get about their business."

Lestrade stared at my friend. "You know what has happened. You know who the thief is."

Holmes waved a hand airily. "I am merely waiting on confirmation of my hypothesis and then we can arrest our over-bold jewel thief. Come, let us speak to these good people."

One of the guards opened the door into the other room. There were about ten people crowded in there. Well-dressed, and in some case, well-connected people. I noticed at least one Member of Parliament and a titled peer. They looked at us expectantly.

"Thank you for being so patient, ladies and gentlemen," Cavanagh said. "Inspector Lestrade of Scotland Yard and Mr. Sherlock Holmes tell me that everything is under control, and you are free to go about your day. I do apologize for holding you up like this."

The M.P. that I had recognized, Freddie Taverner, waved a hand. "I think, sir, that I speak for all of us when I say that it has been a long time since any of us has had such an interesting morning."

Everyone filed out of the room, most stopping to have a word with Holmes. They all seemed thrilled to be involved, even tangentially, with one of his cases. Holmes bore it all stoically, but his relief was obvious when the last of them left the building.

Lestrade looked at my friend. "Well, Holmes, what now?"

"Now, Lestrade?" my friend replied. "Now we wait."

"For what?"

"I sent Wiggins on an errand. We wait to hear from him." With that Holmes walked about to one of the display cases and, to all intents and purposes, became engrossed in studying the small statues that lay within.

Lestrade and I exchanged a look of bewilderment, before Lestrade sighed, and headed for the chair Mrs. Crowther had been sitting on. "If we must wait, I am not doing it standing up. I did too much of that when I was a constable."

I agreed and looked around for another chair. One of the guards brought one over to me. I sank down into it gratefully. Both of us watched Holmes as he continued his study of the contents of the display cases. After a moment, Cavanagh went and joined him, and I could see both men talking amicably. Cavanagh was as passionate about his subject as Holmes was on his. Holmes had told me more than once that someone who knows their subject intimately is always interesting to listen to, even if the subject does not much interest you personally.

It was perhaps half an hour later that we heard the door downstairs open. Holmes turned from the display cases as the inner door opened to admit Wiggins. The lad was clutching a folded sheet of paper in his hand. "'Ere yer go, Mr. 'Olmes. Bloke in Bradford sent a reply back quick smart, 'e did."

Holmes took the paper from Wiggins. "Thank you, Wiggins." He took some more coins from his pocket and gave them to the boy.

"Thankee guvnor. Will yer be needin' our 'elp terday?"

"I do not think so, Wiggins," Holmes said as he read the note. "...but if I few of you would care to hang around the Northumberland Hotel, I would be obliged."

Wiggins raised a grimy fore finger to his temple. "Will do." He turned and slipped back down the stairs.

Holmes looked at Lestrade. "You may wish to send for several more constables. We have arrests to make, and the two you brought with you, and are now at the Northumberland Hotel, may not be enough."

"You are confident of an arrest?" Lestrade said.

Holmes folded the paper he had received and tucked it into his breast pocket. He patted it gently. "Oh yes, Lestrade. Quite confident indeed."

Lestrade dispatched one of the guards, not Wilson this time, to Scotland Yard with a written request for two more constables to meet us outside the Northumberland Hotel.

Holmes frowned, obviously feeling that two more would not be enough, but the set look on Lestrade's face made him hold his tongue.

We waited another half an hour before Holmes gestured to the door. "It is time we were leaving, gentlemen. We have thieves to catch."

The trip to the Northumberland Hotel passed in silence. Cavanagh had insisted on coming with us, saying that the pectoral was his responsibility, and he would like to be there when it was recovered.

There were two constables waiting outside the hotel. Lestrade left them to wait in the reception area, much to the chagrin of the desk clerk, from whom Lestrade had got the Crowther's room number.

Crowther, who had been sitting in a chair by the window, leaped to his feet as we entered the room, closing the door behind us. "Well," he demanded. "Have you found my wife's brooch?"

Holmes shook his head. "I do not believe it was stolen, Mr. Crowther."

"WHAT???" the man's bellow of rage filled the room.

"It is quite clear to me that the 'theft' of the brooch was a distraction from the real theft. That of the pectoral that you erroneously believed was made of rubies. No doubt you slipped the brooch to your 'son'."

"You scoundrel! How dare you impugn me so! I am a businessman of good standing…"

"According to the police in Bradford, you and your lady wife are suspected of numerous jewel thefts. Nor do you have a son. You take in young lads straight from prison, allegedly to give them a chance at an honest life. It is interesting that every single one of these lads were in prison for theft. In the majority of cases, they were imprisoned for the crime of picking pockets."

"It is quite a jump from picking pockets to picking locks," Lestrade observed.

Holmes chuckled drily. "I had yet to get to the best part, Lestrade."

"Which is?" I asked.

"Mr. Crowther's father was a locksmith. The best in Bradford, I am told. Crowther here learned his father's trade, but an accident as a young man broke the middle finger of his left hand to the point of almost crushing it. A locksmith needs the nimble use of both hands. From that point on he was unable to follow in his father's trade."

Lestrade nodded, "But had the knowledge to be able to teach it to others."

"Precisely," Holmes said, "Well done, Lestrade."

Crowther's face had drained of colour. "You can't prove it! It's mere suspicion."

At that point the door opened, and a tall, slender, well-dressed, young man entered the room. He froze when he saw us all.

Lestrade was the first to move. "Well, well, well, if the Dickybird hasn't come home to roost. Welcome back to London, Richard Sikes."

"I ain't done nothin'," the boy protested.

"No? There is the matter of the stolen pectoral?"

"You can't prove that. I ain't got it on me." The boy looked smug.

I wondered what we were going to do. There was no sign of the pectoral in the small room, and I did not think either of the Crowthers were foolish enough to have the item on their persons.

From the top of the wardrobe came a soft meow.

Lestrade looked up. "How did that cat get there?"

The animal jumped gracefully down and sauntered over to Holmes, where she proceeded to rub herself around his ankles in a familiar movement.

"It is Bast," I said. "The cat from the exhibition."

"It can't be," Lestrade exclaimed. "There is no way it could have followed us here and got in without being seen."

The cat walked over to the skirting board next to the wardrobe. She pawed at it briefly and looked back at Holmes. The meow she gave sounded almost like a command.

Holmes walked over and dropped to his knees on the floor. I noticed the Crowthers flinch. As we all focused our attention on Holmes, Sikes whirled around, shoved the two constables out of the way and fled the room. Lestrade shouted and sent one of the constables after him, before turning back to glare at the Crowthers, who wisely remained where they were.

Holmes ignored all the drama behind him. He drew a knife from his pocket and slid the blade under bottom of the board. There was a sharp crack and a section of the skirting board fell away to reveal a cavity in the wall. Holmes reached in and felt around. When he withdrew his hand there was a cloth wrapped bundle in it. He unwrapped the bundle carefully to reveal the stolen pectoral and a cabochon ruby brooch.

Cavanagh let out a great sign. "Oh thank, God."

"Perhaps," Holmes said, with a twinkle in his eye, "You should be thanking Bast instead."

Lestrade looked at Crowther and his wife, both of whom looked as if they wished to follow Sikes, only we stood between them and the door.

Lestrade and the remaining constable handcuffed the two of them before ushering them out of the door. At the doorway, Mrs. Crowther turned her head towards Holmes. "I want my brooch back!"

Holmes chuckled. "Your brooch? I think we shall find that this brooch originally belonged to Lady Hazelmoor. It was stolen when she was visiting Keldleigh Manor, which is, I believe, just outside of Bradford. I remember seeing the name Crowther on the guest list when the Bradford constabulary consulted me on the case."

"I do not remember that," I said with a frown.

Holmes shrugged. "I was unable to assist them at the time. It was at the same time as the little affair of Major Portgrove's music box."

I nodded as I remembered the case; one which I have yet to write about.

Holmes, Cavanagh, and I followed Lestrade and his prisoners downstairs to find pandemonium reigning outside the hotel.

Richard Sikes lay on the ground, being handcuffed by a constable. Wiggins and several of the Irregulars stood nearby looking pleased with themselves.

Wiggins grinned at Holmes. "The little bugger came runnin' out wiv a couple o' rozzers after 'im. Figured yer'd want us ter stop 'im. So, we jumped 'im. Me, an' Timmy, an' Fred, an' Pete."

"Well done, lads." Holmes fairly beamed at them and distributed coins to the four of them. They then slipped away into the gathering crowd.

Sikes was hauled to his feet, his clothes and face filthy from the dirty pavement. He joined the two Crowthers in a police growler, and they were all taken off to Scotland Yard. Lestrade and Cavanagh took a cab and followed them. Cavanagh to tell the story and identify the pectoral formally.

It was late that evening when Lestrade and Cavanagh come to Baker Street to learn exactly how Holmes and worked out who the thieves were.

We sat sipping appreciatively at a fine whisky that had been the gift of a Scottish client.

"So, how did you work it out?" Cavanagh asked.

"There were not a lot of clues, I will admit," said Holmes. "But once it became obvious that Crowther was not a true grain merchant, much became clear."

"Not a true grain merchant?" Lestrade asked.

"The man hated cats," Holmes replied. "No grain merchant hates cats. Indeed, they are grateful for them."

"Of course," cried Cavanagh. "They protect the warehouses from mice and rats. Thereby averting disease. That is one of the reasons Egyptians venerated them."

"Exactly! No man would be so disparaging of an animal that protects his livelihood. Therefore, the role of grain merchant was a way to disguise his source of income."

"Other people's jewels," I said.

Holmes nodded.

"I have been in contact with Inspector Thorpe in Bradford," Lestrade said. "He asked me to pass on his thanks. They have been after the Crowthers for quite some time. And expect some token of thanks from Lady Hazelmoor. She was ecstatic to learn that her ruby brooch had been recovered, and by the great Sherlock Holmes, no less."

"But what about the cat?" I asked. "And the hiding place in the wall?"

"The hiding place is fairly common practice amongst people who stay frequently in the same hotels," Holmes said. "You will find most hotels have little spots like that, created by past visitors."

"The cat must have jumped onto the back of the growler when we left Montague Street," Lestrade said.

"But how did the cat know about the hiding place?" I asked.

Holmes looked at me, a strange smile on his face. "What is my main maxim, Watson?"

I thought for a moment. "When you have eliminated all which is impossible, then whatever remains, however improbable, must be the truth."

Holmes raised his glass to me, "Exactly, my dear Watson!"

Introduction: Why Sherlock Holmes?

I wrote this little essay for David Ruffle's "Sherlock Holmes: Tales from the Stranger's Room Volume 3".

It basically explains why, and how, I became interested in the Great Detective and his world.

"Sherlock Holmes: Tales from the Stranger's Room Volume 3" was published by MX Publishing in 2017.

Why Sherlock Holmes?

I was asked a question recently that got me thinking. I was talking with someone who knows me, but only relatively recently. He was unaware of my dedication to Sherlock Holmes and was surprised when I told him about my story being included in this august volume. He asked me "Why Sherlock Holmes? Why that character, and not, say, Hercule Poirot?" I made a flippant remark and left it at that, but he really did get me thinking on the subject of my exposure to the Great Detective.

I can still remember the first Sherlock Holmes story I read. I was at my local library, desperately looking for something to read. I'd exhausted all the children's books, and my poor mother had had to join the library so I could get adult books to read. I was ten years old. This day, I was wandering disconsolately among the shelves unable to make a choice. The librarian, a neighbour of ours, took pity on me. She marched to the shelves, selected a book and handed it to me with the prophetic words "I know you'll enjoy this."

Doubtfully, I looked at the cover. It was 'A Study in Scarlet'. I checked it out at took it home. Settling down to read it, I wasn't too enthralled, until I came to the passage where Stamford is explaining to Watson about Holmes beating a dead body with a stick to ascertain whether bruises can form after death. That was it. I was hooked. And when it got to the line "You have been in Afghanistan, I perceive", I was not only hooked, but reeled in and gaffed as well. The story was exciting, and intelligent, and the heroes were interesting. I say heroes, because it was immediately obvious to me that Holmes and Watson were a pair. You couldn't have one without the other. Poirot can survive without his Hastings, but Holmes without Watson is like meat without salt.

I was back up at the library the next day to see if there were any more of these treasures. I happily carried home the library's entire collection of Sherlock Holmes stories. Seeing my enthusiasm, my father's Christmas gift to me that year was an omnibus edition of all the stories.

Why Sherlock Holmes? On the face of it a Victorian detective should hold no charms for a 20th century child growing into a 21st century woman. It's a question I have asked myself over and over again for the last 40 years. I've also realized that it isn't just a question for me. It is almost a universal question.

Holmes and Watson made an early transition to movies and to radio. For many people of a certain age, the first names they associate with the pairing is Basil Rathbone and Nigel Bruce. Then television, and Granada's wonderful adaptations of the canon with Jeremy Brett and David Burke/Edward Hardwicke, became the Holmes and Watson(s) for another generation. And the beat goes on. Each new Sherlock Holmes movie announcement is guaranteed an excited audience, whether for Robert Downey Junior, or Will Ferrell. There are TWO television partnerships with Benedict Cumberbatch and

Martin Freeman in London, and Johnny Lee Miller and Lucy Liu in New York.

Then there is publishing. More pastiches have been published now than the original canon. Sherlock Holmes is there in traditional Arthur Conan Doyle style stories, in steampunk novels, or battling Lovecraft's eldritch gods. Every year I read at least ten new Sherlock Holmes books.

Finally, there is merchandise. Not just tie in stuff to the BBC's version, but much to be gathered and treasured by the dedicated Sherlockian. I have a tee shirt with a Sherlock Holmes quote on it purchased from the British Library, postcards of some of Sidney Paget's illustrations purchased from the Museum of London, and not to mention my highly prized Sherlock Holmes rubber duck. I cannot think of any other literary creations that have spawned as much memorabilia as Holmes and Watson.

So, the question remains: Why Sherlock Holmes?

It isn't the mysteries. Other writers have created stories as beguiling and as interesting as any Arthur Conan Doyle did. Agatha Christie's 'Murder on the Orient Express' is a good case. At no point did Sherlock Holmes have to deal with a case where, quite literally, everybody did it. Margery Allingham's Albert Campion, and Dorothy L. Sayers' Lord Peter Wimsey all solved interesting and intricate mysteries. But none of them, not even Agatha Christie, has generated the level of obsession with the characters.

It certainly isn't the continuity, or lack thereof. Arthur Conan Doyle is pretty much a by word for how not to create a fictional world. Mrs. Hudson mysteriously morphs into Mrs. Turner in one story! He cannot seem to remember if Watson's first name is John or James! And please do NOT get me started on Watson's wonderful wandering war wound!

It isn't the depth of the supporting characters either because most of them are pretty one dimensional. Holmes and Watson fairly blaze off the pages, leaving all the other characters in shadow. Even firm fan favourite Mrs. Hudson doesn't get much of a look in in the original stories. It took movies and television to flesh her out. Irene Handl in 'The Private Life of Sherlock Holmes' and Una Stubbs in BBC's 'Sherlock' are arguably the two portrayals that have given this character the most life.

So, what is left? What is it that makes Sherlock Holmes so readable, relatable, and thoroughly enjoyable as much in the 21st century as it was in the 19th?

The answer, to me, is friendship.

It seems to me that Sherlock Holmes and John Watson are archetypes for friendship. The friendship the characters had formed by the end of 'A Study in Scarlet' drew me in. I mentioned Poirot and Hastings before. Hastings is the sidekick. He is there to provide an audience for Poirot's brilliance. Hastings is not an equal partner in the enterprise. It is the same in many other detective pairings. But not with Holmes and

Watson. You cannot have one without the other. Holmes says it himself: "I would be lost without my Boswell."

It is possibly the most intense friendship in literature. It is the friendship we all secretly desire. Someone who would give their life for us, and that we would do the same for. It is a friendship shown most clearly in that most moving of passages from 'The Adventure of the Three Garridebs':

"My friend's wiry arms were around me and he was leading me to the chair. "You're not hurt, Watson? For God's sake say that you're not hurt!" It was worth a wound - it was worth many wounds - to know the depth of loyalty and love which lay beyond that cold mask. The clear, hard eyes were dimmed for a moment, and the firm lips were shaking. For the one and only time I caught a glimpse of a great heart as well as of a great brain."

It's a friendship that has the ring of truth about it, based as it is on honesty. Holmes and Watson both have their vices and virtues. One of their earliest exchanges in 'A Study in Scarlet' has both men laying forth their worst habits: *"Let me see—what are my other shortcomings. I get in the dumps at times, and don't open my mouth for days on end. You must not think I am sulky when I do that. Just let me alone, and I'll soon be right. What have you to confess now? It's just as well for two fellows to know the worst of one another before they begin to live together."*

I laughed at this cross-examination. "I keep a bull pup," I said, "and I object to rows because my nerves are shaken, and I get up at all sorts of ungodly hours, and I am extremely lazy. I have another set of vices when I'm well, but those are the principal ones at present."

Of course Holmes failed to mention several other habits, as Watson notes in 'The Musgrave Ritual' for example: *"I have always held, too, that pistol practice should be distinctly an open-air pastime; and when Holmes, in one of his queer humours, would sit in an armchair with his hair-trigger and a hundred Boxer cartridges and proceed to adorn the opposite wall with a patriotic V.R. done in bullet pocks, I felt strongly that neither the atmosphere nor the appearance of our room was improved by it."*

Strong onscreen chemistry between various Holmes and Watsons has helped keep the character's flame alive. Jeremy Brett and David Burke, followed by Jeremy Brett and Edward Hardwicke had perfect onscreen vibes. In later years Robert Downey Junior and Jude Law sparkled on the big screen. And the chemistry between Benedict Cumberbatch and Martin Freeman can only be described as superb.

Sherlock Holmes and John Watson are two people who understand each other perfectly. It's not a perfect friendship, no friendship is, but it is, I think, an ideal that people aspire to. A friendship based on loyalty, trust, humour, and love. We all want it, and because it is so rare, we find stories about such a pair of friends to be irresistible. The relationship that is friendship hasn't changed in hundreds of years, leaving the

Sherlock Holmes stories as strong and as fresh as when they first appeared in Strand Magazine.

Afterword

Thank you for reading. I hope you enjoyed the stories.

If you want to say hello, please come and find me in the following places:

Twitter: @EspineuxAlpha

Facebook: https://www.facebook.com/Margaret-Walsh-Author-194040130606431

Tumblr: https://www.tumblr.com/blog/margysmusings

GoodReads: https://www.goodreads.com/author/show/19048093.Margaret_Walsh

MX Publishing

MX Publishing brings the best in new Sherlock Holmes novels, biographies, graphic novels and short story collections every month. With over 500 books it's the largest catalogue of new Sherlock Holmes books in the world.

We have over one hundred and fifty Holmes authors. The majority of our authors write new Holmes fiction - in all genres from very traditional pastiches through to modern novels, fantasy, crossover, children's books and humour.

In Holmes biography we have award winning historians including Alistair Duncan. Brian Pugh and Maureen Whittaker who have all won the Sherlock Holmes Book of The Year Award.

MX Publishing also has one of the largest communities of Holmes fans on Facebook and Twitter under @mxpublishing.

MX is a social enterprise that has raised over $100,000 for good causes including Happy Life Mission (Kenya), Undershaw School for children with learning disabilities (UK) and the WFP (World Food Programme).

www.mxpublishing.com

Also from MX Publishing

The Detective and The Woman Series

 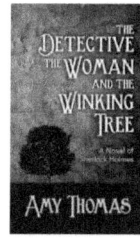  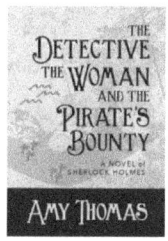

The Detective and The Woman

The Detective, The Woman and The Winking Tree

The Detective, The Woman and The Silent Hive

The Detective, The Woman and The Pirate's Bounty

"The book is entertaining, puzzling and a lot of fun. I believe the author has hit on the only type of long-term relationship possible for Sherlock Holmes and Irene Adler. The details of the narrative only add force to the romantic defects we expect in both of them and their growth and development are truly marvelous to watch. This is not a love story. Instead, it is a coming-of-age tale starring two of our favorite characters."

Philip K Jones

www.mxpublishing.com

Also from MX Publishing

When the papal apartments are burgled in 1901, Sherlock Holmes is summoned to Rome by Pope Leo XII. After learning from the pontiff that several priceless cameos that could prove compromising to the church, and perhaps determine the future of the newly unified Italy, have been stolen, Holmes is asked to recover them. In a parallel story, Michelangelo, the toast of Rome in 1501 after the unveiling of his Pieta, is commissioned by Pope Alexander VI, the last of the Borgia pontiffs, with creating the cameos that will bedevil Holmes and the papacy four centuries later. For fans of Conan Doyle's immortal detective, the game is always afoot. However, the great detective has never encountered an adversary quite like the one with whom he crosses swords in "The Vatican Cameos.."

"An extravagantly imagined and beautifully written Holmes story"
(**Lee Child**, NY Times Bestselling author, Jack Reacher series)

Also from MX Publishing

The Conan Doyle Notes (The Hunt For Jack The Ripper)
"Holmesians have long speculated on the fact that the Ripper murders aren't mentioned in the canon, though the obvious reason is undoubtedly the correct one: even if Conan Doyle had suspected the killer's identity he'd never have considered mentioning it in the context of a fictional entertainment. Ms Madsen's novel equates his silence with that of the dog in the night-time, assuming that Conan Doyle did know who the Ripper was but chose not to say – which, of course, implies that good old stand-by, the government cover-up. It seems unlikely to me that the Ripper was anyone famous or distinguished, but fiction is not fact, and "The Conan Doyle Notes" is a gripping tale, with an intelligent, courageous and very likable protagonist in DD McGil."
The Sherlock Holmes Society of London

www.mxpublishing.com

Also from MX Publishing

The Sun and Shadow Series – Tracy Revels

Shadowfall, Shadowblood, Shadowwraith

In the strange beginning to a very strange adventure the illustrious personage who arrives at 221B Baker Street is Titatnia, Queen of the Fairies. Irene Adler is a soul-stealing monster, young Stamford is a zombie, and John Brown is a supernatural guardian. The abduction of a body from Highgate Cemetery and the disappearance of the London Stone are simply a prelude the theft of England's most sacred relic, the heart of St. George. Dr. Revels has researched deeply into English legend and Shadowfall has a delirious, almost surrealist quality, like an enjoyable nightmare.

Sherlock Holmes Society of London reviews Shadowfall

9 781787 059962